The Pathfinder Collection

Stories from the Inner Sea

H. Rad Bethlen

Rooster & Raven

roosterandravenpublishing.com
hradbethlen.com

For the Daughters of Zeus and Mnemosyne

Author Statement Concerning Artificial Intelligence

The way I write consist of several phases.

1. Idea generation.
2. Research.
3. Story development.
4. Outlining.
5. Writing the rough draft.
6. Editing and rewriting.
7. Editing and polishing.
8. Copy editing.

I will *occasionally* use AI during the research phase if I can't locate some bit of information on my own—but I try to locate it on my own first.

I will *occasionally* use AI during the story's development if I get stuck on something—but I try to resolve my own story issues first.

I *intentionally* use AI during the copy editing phase as a stand-in for a copy editor, which I can't afford to pay for yet which I don't want to go without.

A copy editor is the last set of eyes to look at a manuscript to check for grammar, usage, spelling, and punctuation mistakes. I ask the AI copy editor to make suggestions on corrections. I evaluate those suggestions. If I agree, I make the changes.

I don't use AI for anything else.

Be comforted that these stories were written by a human being for other human beings.

H. Rad Bethlen

Introduction

When I began to teach myself to tell stories in the written form I took a brute force approach. I forced myself to face the blank page and put words on it that told stories. I didn't wait for the muse. I didn't make excuses. I didn't allow myself to succumb to my own fears. I was demanding, I was driven.

John Gardner, in *On Becoming a Novelist,* said:

> Drivenness only helps if it forces the writer not to suicide but to the making of splendid works of art, allowing him indifference to whether or not the novels sell, whether or not it is appreciated. Drivenness is trouble for both the novelist and his friends; but no novelist, I think, can succeed without it. Along with the peasant in the novelist, there must be a man with a whip.

Taking a brute force approach meant that I had to find inspiration wherever I could. I got the inspiration for the first story I sold from a line in a short story by Ambrose Bierce. It wasn't an important line, but it had mood. That was enough.

The *Pathfinder Campaign Setting: The Inner Sea World Guide* was a source of many short stories and even a novel (*Breaking the Reign of the Dead*). Not all of those short stories are collected here. A few are still in the process of being edited and refined. I hope to release them when they're ready for the world.

My hope is that these stories breathe life into the Inner Sea region. If you tell stories in the Inner Sea, if your characters roam there, may they meet Captain Brindisi or

Old Khalden. It makes me smile to think they will. Until that day, I hope you'll read these stories and enjoy them.

H. Rad Bethlen

The Preservation of Captain Haifa Brindisi

Being a record of tragedy, found in the wreckage of the sailing ship Dragon's Star; *which, having been damaged while at sea and later smashed amongst rocks in the Ironbound Archipelago, was the scene of much suffering.*

Let this stand as a testament to the weakness of the body, the capriciousness of the mind, and tell that the soul does suffer both. I am the only survivor of the ship *Dragon's Star*. I was born and raised in the fishing village of Arsmeril, on the northern coast of Varisia. My father was from Ustalav, having fled the curse of that soil. Nay, he did not suffer any soil, but passed from land to sea, to be seen no more. What I have of him is precious little; although, it can now be said, and you shall come to believe, that he did not leave me bereft of the gifts of his blood.

I was raised by my mother and uncles, simple fisherfolk; hearty, silent, and devout to the gods. I learned by heart *The Eight Scrolls* and can recite from memory the *Hymns to the Wind and the Waves,* being often of the necessity to call upon the guidance of Desna and the mercy of Gozreh.

I have many male cousins, but none were so by nature drawn to sea than I, and although I was a girl, my uncles did not keep me back, seeing that salt was in my blood. By the time I could balance enough to walk I had my sea legs. While the other girls of the village dreamt of the Eagle Knights of Andoran, or some suchlike romance, I was longing for open seas and fair winds.

If I had known what my fate would be, that I would not sail at the pleasure of fair winds, not at all, but be put meanly to land by the cruelest winds any sailor has suffered, I would that an Eagle Knight had taken me away and kept me in his castle, a pretty bauble, safe from all knowledge of sea and self.

Know that we suffered from a total want of all that would sustain life. The *Dragon's Star* had been battered by waves and was leaking profusely. We had endured relentless winds, which had the sinister nature of the fey. Indeed, we worried that some sea spirit was revenging us for an unknown injury.

First, two pair of our foremost main shrouds on the larboard side were taken by the wind. The next morning our two fore main shrouds on the starboard side were carried away. We applied runner and tackle for the security of the mast. The weather was intolerably bad, day and night. By the next morning the wind calmed. We sang hymns and made offerings to Gozreh. Despite this, the next day a sudden wind came and, to our unspeakable horror, tore clean away the forestay and foresheets. Not only this, the foresail was rent in pieces. We had no recourse and tried our best under a balanced reefed mainsail.

The sea was as mountains upon us and it was here that the ship began to leak in earnest, the wood strained beyond its natural constitution. That night the tack of our square sail gave way. The sail was torn to tatters. Our flying jib was blown overboard. Despite all this we made way, our only bit of canvas being our mainsail. Our ship sat low due to the water we'd taken on. We worked the pumps without respite. Gozreh was not finished. After a calm that put us at ease, a gale blew hard from SSE and took apart our mainsail. We were at his mercy.

. . .

The *Dragon's Star* sailed out of Magnimar. We'd a load destined for Promise, on the island of Hermea; yes, the home of the great gold dragon, Mengkare, or so it's said, none I know of having seen him. We'd made the port once before and little can be known of the city, for a high, red sandstone wall and gates of burnished bronze keep all within secured against intrusion from outside. We were blown NNW and figured ourselves closer to the Mordant Spire or Syranita's Aerie then Promise; although, we had no way of knowing, having no sight of stars, nor sun, nor land.

A great deal of our stores were flooded, despite our efforts to preserve them. Much of the cargo was of no use. We had only some small amount of flour, sugar, dried meat, raisins, wine, but precious little fresh water. We rationed these but my men, against orders, took the wine to excess and the rationing was forgotten. The storms raged and we knew not which way the wind took us. If we passed beyond the Mordant Spire all was lost, for no ships sail those waters.

We had among us a priest of Gozreh, Timmons, who we adorned with the title of Saint. He was an old sailor of many campaigns. He had seen the Eye of Abendego and many other wonders. He'd been shipwrecked twice before, the second time suffering forty-one days on a barren island. He was of great aid to us. Not only was he immune to the hardships of the sea, he could provide food and fresh water by means of divine largesse. We could scarcely believe our misfortune—and his—when a wave took him overboard and carried him out of reach. He disappeared, and with him our hope.

I cautioned the men against wine, for it does little to aid under such circumstances. They refused to drink the water, convinced it was brackish. The wine being more plentiful, they preferred it. What little water there was I retained, it being my only advantage against Fate. The men were constantly warming the wine, for which they maintained a small fire. It got so that the smell of it was noxious to me.

We'd been thirteen days at the mercy of the storm, tossed terribly, half-sunk, and without means, when I retired to my cabin to await the arrival of Trelmarixian, the Horseman of Famine, for he was surely stalking us. By this time I was emaciated with sickness. Despite having hooks in the water there came no fish. I kept within arms-length only this journal, an ink pot and quill, the dirty water, and Saint Timmon's wand. I must tell of this.

Timmons had fashioned a wand out of an oar that he had with him when he'd been forty-one days upon the rock. The oar, his trousers, and his shirt, were all that had come with him from the wreckage of the *Ruby Prince*. This oar was his means of survival and rescue. He used it to club turtles and crack their shells. He resorted to drinking their blood, there being no fresh water on the island, and gathering their meat by use of sharp-edged stones. He found the highest point and planted his oar, using his shirt as a flag. A ship, the *Kantaria,* which had been blown off course, saw the shirt-flag and sent a boat to investigate.

Timmons brought his oar from that desperate place and, feeling a certain affection for it, whittled it down to something manageable. This he enchanted with all sorts of useful magics. One of its enchantments was the calling down of a pillar of fire, which proved a deterrent to piracy. This wand was in his quarters when he was taken by the sea. I retrieved it, more to preserve the old man's memory, than to make use of, for I had no learning of magic and knew not how to operate it.

. . .

After a fortnight of hard blowing, the sea calmed. We were adrift. The men came and said they were hungry and having no recourse were going to draw lots to see which among them would sacrifice himself to preserve the rest. They wished my blessing on this demonic pact. Perceiving them in liquor, I begged them to wait out the day, hoping that our deliverance would come presently. They argued my request, saying what had to be done best be done now and why prolong our suffering.

They said they'd eaten all the leather belonging to the pumps, cut their shoes to strips and eaten those, and had even eaten the buttons from their coats. I warned them against the damage such an act would do to their everlasting souls. I beseeched them to pray. They said there was hunger to contend with, damn prayer. They said they cared not if I acquiesced, having come to me out of respect for my former responsibility as captain, although they contended that circumstances had made all equal.

I told them I would never condone such an abhorrent act and while I could do little in opposition I would not give the order nor partake of their sinful feast. They responded that they required not an order and as to eating or not eating, I was free to follow my own inclination. They left but soon returned and said that they'd come together and drawn lots.

Know this, of those left all were human with one half-elf, who had been my steward, his name being Melorca. They said that the lot had fallen upon him. He flung himself at my feet, pleading that I do something, but I was powerless. The men drug him from my cabin. The manner in which they'd previously gone away to converse amongst themselves, and how the lot had fallen, gave me the idea that the half-elf had been sorely treated. Although, in all honesty, it surprised me that they'd even pretended to treat him as equal to themselves.

They dragged him to the steerage and pierced his neck at the base of the skull. This I was told of later. They cut him open and began to extract his entrails, wishing to fry them for dinner. One man, Dorset, was so taken with hunger he cut out Melorca's liver and ate it then and there, despite the fire being at-hand. He paid for his impatience.

That night he went raving mad and was thrown overboard by the others, this, despite their wish to preserve the meat of his body. They were fearful of gaining his condition, should they partake of him.

That evening I heard one of the men say to the others, "Even though she would not consent our getting of meat, let us give her some." One of them entered my cabin with a piece of Melorca's flesh, and offered it to me. I raised the wand and said I'd rather burn him to Hell and the ship with him, then resort to such an act, and further dared him to return a second time with such an offering.

Despite their earlier excesses with both wine and stores, the men rationed Melorca's remains with the greatest of care. All this time I ate nothing, only sipping now and again of the water. Knowing that I had condemned them, and knowing too that their hunger should return, I expected some violence to my person. I slept little and kept Timmon's wand in-hand—as a bluff.

A few days after the last of Melorca had been consumed they returned to my cabin. They said they had seen nothing of land nor sail, had caught no fish, had no fresh water, and nothing else which would sustain life. They again asked for my blessing over the choosing of lots. Furthermore, they argued that all this time I had partaken of no sustenance and surely must be too weak to remain stubborn.

I argued against another act of murder. What good had the half-elf's death done them, for they were once more hungry and desperate? They said lots must be drawn. Seeing as I could do nothing to prevent it, and seeing how unfair their earlier selection had been, I tore a sheet from this journal into pieces and wrote everyone's name upon a fragment. These went into a can from which I drew a name.

The man whose name it was, El-Barek, a sailor who had come from far away Rahadoum, a man of great fortitude, beseeched his fellows: "I ask no god to help me, for they've done enough to damn us all. I ask only for five minutes to reflect upon my life." This was granted to him. Afterwards, he walked willingly into the steerage and met the same fate as Melorca.

I had suffered more than I ever thought I could endure. I had found a state well beyond weakness. I could barely keep my eyes open or grip my pen. It has taken every effort to keep up a journal.

I drank the last of the water, closed my eyes, and prepared to die. Some time later, I know not how long, I awoke with a greater thirst than I previously had. There was a rich taste upon my tongue. I found the strength to sit up. Beside me was one of my men, Hoskuld, an Ulfen. He held a wooden bowl in his hands, filled with blood.

"Quiet," he said. "Trelmarixian is close. Protest not, for it is too late. Drink." With this he held the bowl to my lips. I drank. I drank not only that single bowl of El-Barek's blood but many. I slept well for the first time in memory and was so completely restored that I was able to leave my bed and walk amongst my men. Indeed, I was so fully restored that I felt not at all the ill effects of starvation, nor of dehydration. The men gazed at me as if I were a miracle. Even though they had consumed Melorca and were now consuming El-Barek, they had little health, keeping just out of reach of the Horseman.

The sky was clear, the sun especially bright. I found that it pained me to remain under it. I found also the smell of El-Barek's cooking flesh to be revolting. The aroma coming from the pail of his blood, however, was so agreeable that before I was aware of myself I was drawing it out with cupped hands and drinking as a glutton.

This made the men wary. They offered me meat but I declined. I was aware of their judgment and returned to my cabin. I licked and sucked every crevice of my hand's flesh. The taste of blood was intoxicating. I sat on my bunk in a state of unwholesome wellness. It was a pleasure to be out of the sunlight.

Despite all I had drunk, I could not refrain from obsessing over El-Barek's blood. I began to jealously desire it for myself. That evening, as soon as the sun fell below the horizon, I went to the deck and found the pail empty. This aggrieved me more than reason would suggest. I was furious and kicked the men awake to inquire if they'd thrown the blood overboard. No, they said, they drank it. I began to accuse them but caught myself and returned to my cabin.

I was too agitated for sleep. I felt that I'd been wronged by my men. I believed that El-Barek's blood was mine. I was in a near frenzy when I came to myself. Where had such thoughts come from? Was I truly so desiring of human blood that I planned vengeance upon those who had denied me?

It was then that I understood why I had been so completely restored by El-Barek's blood. I understood why my father, who I always thought dishonorable, had not stayed to raise me, but had taken a boat and gone alone upon the water never to return. I understood that it was not the cursed soil of Ustalav that my father fled from, but the curse within himself. My father, although he had once been, was not human, nor was I entirely human, and had *never* been. They've a term for my kind, a term told in stories to frighten children, a dhampier. The living offspring of a vampire. A live-born undead.

I barricaded myself in my cabin, fearful that the craving for blood was too powerful a lure. I feared not my men, I feared for them. In time my men came to the door, beat upon it, and announced "land ho." I freed myself and went to the deck. Indeed, there was land. We rejoiced. Here might be civilization and with it hope. If not people and their works, may there at least be fresh water and wild nature with all her bounty. We were at the mercy of the wind and waves. We had not even oars, we used prayer instead. As if by miracle, the waves carried us to the island.

Yet, the miracle failed. As we approached we saw that the island was barren rock. Worse than this, we were being carried toward it with haste. There was no shore upon which to make a safe landing, only sharp rocks. We braced for impact.

. . .

The ship was smashed upon the rocks. We made our way onto the island. It was but little larger than the *Dragon's Star* and completely devoid of life. Nor was there a spring. There were some divots and natural bowls which we cleaned out in the hope that rainfall would fill them with fresh water enough to drink. Each man watched his divot as if water would appear by necessity alone. Would we once again resort to lots? Not I, for I was twice as strong as all my men combined and could overpower them.

No, there would be no lots. There would be no killing of one to preserve the rest. My men were for *me*. They held my nourishment within. All the blood on that island was mine and would be used to keep me alive until the time when Desna, the goddess of luck and travelers, should vouchsafe my deliverance. If she did not, then the blood of my men would serve only to prolong my misery, nothing more. As to *their* misery, was I not relieving it?

. . .

The last man was two weeks dead when I accepted the will of the gods. I sucked his blood until it was no more. His body was so drained, so light, being only bones and flesh, it caught the wind and sailed when I kicked it from the rock. I was reduced to my previous state, one of utter weakness. Once more did the Horseman of Famine, that prince of starvation, stalk me. I had done all for naught; sacrificed my soul, my salvation, and secured eternal damnation, for what? A few extra weeks of life upon a barren rock.

. . .

I was in the ship when I heard a voice. The remains of the *Dragon's Star* had been tossed high enough on the rocks to remain out of the water, and thus had drained. It was the only place of shade and, while certainly not comfortable, it was the only respite afforded me. I was near death and thought myself delirious, when one man inquired of another, "Signs of life?" I turned my head to gaze out of a hole. I saw a man pass by. He was studying the wreckage but had not seen me, sunk in the gloom.

I thought him a delusion and dismissed all thoughts of rescue; which, I had long abandoned in favor of death. Yet the voices continued. I crawled free of the wreckage and saw that a boat rowed close. Five men sat within, fresh, young, well-fed, and shocked to see me. They had come from a ship at anchor, to which they pointed. I saw the King's colors, King Eodred of Korvosa. I was saved.

. . .

I pen these last words with haste. I must leave my record here, in the *Dragon's Star*. I dare not take it with me, for fear of being found out. Can I digest human food, or must I now, and forever, subsist on human blood? I shall learn while aboard the *Belde,* for that is the name of the ship.

I will say nothing to my rescuers of what has transpired, or of how I managed to outlive my men. It is enough to know that I leave the truth to rot upon this barren rock as the gods left me. I shall pray no more, but, like El-Barek, whose blood awakened me, I shall exercise my own reason, rely upon my own strength, a strength which has saved me while the gods remained aloof and uncaring. I shall go to Ustalav, to learn what I truly am, or perhaps to distant Geb, where I need not fear.

Haifa Brindisi,
Captain of the *Dragon's Star*

The Love of El-Barek

"Let us speak," said El-Barek. "Or, allow me to speak. Will you listen?"

"Aye," said Hoskuld, an Ulfen, who had, as a young man, rowed free of the ice-choked fjords of the Linnorm Kings to live upon the water ever since. This was the first voyage the two had made together—and would be the last either would make—yet, amongst the crew, it was the Ulfen that El-Barek was most fond of. He had found, despite the superstitious nature of the Ulfen people, being especially pronounced in his shipmate, that they shared something in common. It was an oft spoke refrain that: "A Rahadoumi laughs at death—but it is a shared laugh, not a defiant one." He knew the Ulfen felt the same; albeit, more defiant than shared.

The two shipwrecked sailers went below deck. Hoskuld sat upon a barrel that had become wedged amongst what remained of the smashed and ruined cargo. El-Barek stood, feet apart, arms crossed over his chest. Neither felt the bite of the wind, that, having gathered the chill from the plains of Icemark, blew through the gaps in the boards.

Both were emaciated, their features made sharp. The reddish-blonde had drained from Hoskuld's chin whiskers, just as the warm-ochre had drained from El-Barek's flesh. Slow death had turned them gray. They wore far less than they would have liked. Their coats were without buttons and hung open. They were barefoot, having long ago cut their shoes into strips, boiled these in wine, and eaten them. Even the wine was a memory. The boat rose and dropped on the waves. It had lost its sails weeks prior and was more wreckage than ship.

El-Barek had requested a moment to contemplate the meaning of his life, for he was preparing to die. They had drawn lots, the doomed sailors of the *Dragon's Star*. He was to die so that the others might consume him and live. They had done the same to one prior; a half-elf named Melorca, who, in El-Barek's eyes, had not shown courage when called upon to make the ultimate sacrifice.

El-Barek found it inadequate to reflect alone and in silence. He did not desire a priest, being of Rahadoum, and therefore godless, and besides, the priest had been washed overboard. All he wished was for one who might understand to listen.

"I have no sins to confess," he began. "Nor have I regrets." Hoskuld did not speak, but looked on, his blue eyes sunk deep. El-Barek continued. "I *have* been in love. It is of that I wish to speak." He paused, not knowing how to begin. He began obtusely. "In my homeland, before the gods were banished, there was a Caliph by the name of Abdelraham. He was great because he brought peace to the land and prosperity to the people. He was a loving father to all. He was cultured and wrote sublime verse. He caused much fine architecture to be erected, many temples; which, after his time, were pulled down.

"I've read his memoirs. In them he says, that although he reigned three decades in peace and prosperity, and had the respect and love of his people, and the respect of the genie-folk; who came to his court from lands of brass, of coral, and from cities built of cloud-stuff; although he had all this, including every want of riches and pleasure, and a harem of which the gods were jealous, he had diligently counted the days of genuine happiness that had come to him, and found them to be fourteen."

Hoskuld snorted. El-Barek couldn't help but smile.

"I myself have had twice as many," El-Barek said. "It seems, now that death is at hand, and I've an entire life to reflect upon, I can think of nothing but those brief, bewildering days of passion."

"Tell of her."

"She was fey-blooded," said El-Barek. "Had she come from that great and mysterious oasis, the Eternal Oasis? Or had she come down from the Napsune Mountains, a heavenly bird forced to land? Or had she come from some distant and unknown world, authored before ours, and having been so, is changeable, as was she? She would not say. Although I was madly in love with her, I knew nothing about her."

"Makes it worse," said Hoskuld.

"The words you speak are more true than you know," said El-Barek. "She had hair the color of the fire's dancing flames and eyes like turquoise stones seen through pure water. Her skin was as golden sand under a white-hot sun. To touch it was pleasure and pain."

"Aye."

"Pain," continued El-Barek, "because one could never touch her enough, or deeply enough, and always there is an end to touching, for one cannot subsist on love alone. In her absence there is longing for her, and the desire to touch her again, and no amount of camaraderie, laughter, or good work can fill the void she's left."

Both men reflected upon this.

"A fey-blooded woman is a difficult thing for a man of Rahadoum to contemplate," said El-Barek. "For the men of Rahadoum, the women, too, are of a pragmatic bent, live by a pragmatic philosophy. We must, we've no aid from gods. The fey-blooded are beyond philosophy. Contemplation can make nothing of them. They are alive. So very alive! What can a man's mind make of such abundance of life in the woman he loves? To dwell on it makes him drunk. Argh!"

Hoskuld smiled, despite his hunger and the weariness in his body.

"She loved to listen," continued El-Barek, "and would stare at me with the wide-eyed wonder of a child as I spilled out every precious memory to her. Her questions were poignant. She drove to the heart of the matter always, to the emotion, to the very essence of experience itself. I felt more alive recounting my days to her than I did in the living of them."

"Ha!"

"I poured myself into her. She proved a bottomless vessel. She loved to feel the warmth of the sand just after the sun sets and the air grows cool. Also, the coolness of the sand just as the sun rises and the air grows warm. These dusk and dawn sands were ours. We made love on them, lying on the pelts of predators.

"I spoke of my childhood, of my father and his many voyages, of my mother and sisters. I spoke of my youth, of my fights and flights of fancy, of the girls I pined for and the wizened scholars who filled my head with man's accumulated truths. I had tried my luck as an adventurer, seen all manner of beasts and dangers. When a Chelaxian summoned a devil from Hell, he put a stop to my lust for fame and fortune, but not adventure. I took to the sea, as my father before me. It was during a rare stay on land that I met her.

"We spent twenty-eight days of pure happiness together at the edge of the Eternal Oasis, where no man or care disturbed us." El-Barek fell silent.

"What happened?" asked Hoskuld.

"I reached for her one night, the stars above like cold, distant hearts, the logs of the fire aglow but no longer aflame—"

"Gone?"

El-Barek gazed for a long time into his past. "Yes. I searched for her, in that jungle-like wood about the oasis. I searched the dunes. I searched the heavens. There was no sign of her. If it were not for her fragrance on the furs, for the lingering touch of her at my fingertips, if it were not for her breath on mine, I would believe she had never been."

Hoskuld waited, seeing that El-Barek was not yet done.

"Something more was gone," said El-Barek.

"Yes?"

"A piece of me, of course, my heart, my love, my happiness, these things she'd taken, as the poets say," he flashed his eyes at Hoskuld, "yet, something—more."

Hoskuld studied the other man's face.

"When I came out of the wood and ran into the desert I saw what was missing, no, I *did not see* what had always been." He looked hard at Hoskuld. "My shadow—gone."

"You mean—what do you mean?"

"I cast no shadow, still, to this day," said El-Barek.

"But—"

"You've never noticed. None have. A ship is a poor place for shadow-watching. The sails cast deeper shadows. The ship is always being tossed about. Besides, a sailor's eyes are never on his feet but up in the shrouds or out over the horizon. His feet must take care of themselves."

Hoskuld looked down at El-Barek's feet but the two men were below deck and what little light they had was insufficient for shadow-casting. He rose, grabbed his friend by the arm, and pulled him up onto the deck. He gazed for a long time at the sunlit spot beneath El-Barek.

"One hardly thinks of shadows," said Hoskuld, his voice little above a whisper. "One never looks," he lifted his eyes and met El-Barek's. "She took your shadow?"

"I don't know," said El-Barek. "I can't comprehend it. When I went below, to think about my life, to pour over my memories in search of meaning, I could remember only her. She left a few scraps behind, yes, unimportant details, of my life prior to her," he held out his hands, "almost nothing remains."

"Not fey-blooded," growled Hoskuld, "a true fey."

"Yes."

"By Torag," said Hoskuld, "what's to protect a man's mind against such magic?"

"My mind?" El-Barek laughed. "I've little concern for my mind. My heart—" He saw the other men approaching. They had hunger and impatience in their eyes.

"It's time," called one.

"I'm ready," said El-Barek. He turned to Hoskuld. "If I may impose further, friend?"

"Anything."

"The Captain, she condemns us. She prays when she should eat. She waits for deliverance when she should take action." He glanced toward the closed door to her quarters, then back to Hoskuld. "When I'm dead, take my blood to her and make her drink. Tell her it's water, if you must. She will die without." He glanced above, to the heavens. "The gods have forsaken her." He looked at Hoskuld and the others. "All of you. As for me, I don't want their help and wouldn't take it." He turned back to Hoskuld. "Will you do as I ask?" Hoskuld nodded. "Then there is no more need for words."

Crippled

Rastagar's porcelain mask was chill against his face. He pulled the fur-trimmed hood of his cloak up over his long, red hair. He was standing at the edge of the elevator, the only safe way down into the Forgotten Track.

The massive wooden beams of the elevator pressed from overhead. The thick rope—slack and hanging in great loops over the edge of the cliff—gave one the idea of plunging toward unthinkable pain and death.

He stood with his top lieutenants. Their masks too were conduits of cold. The man to his left held a torch. The crack and pop of the resin was the only sound. Snow fell in large flakes. Their crystalline structures could be studied as they floated down from the evening gloom into the globe of flickering light.

"How can we be certain?" asked the torchbearer. "The storm—"

"The messenger promised nothing would stop them," answered Rastagar.

The messenger had come that morning, racing ahead of the storm, and had departed with equal dispatch, determined to keep his lead.

Rastagar had read and reread the letter. A higher ranking Mask was coming. He was ordered to make himself *obsequious*. He had to ask what the word meant. Thankfully, someone knew. A higher ranking Mask? In all his years running the penal colony/mine no Mask from Thronestep had ever taken an interest. The looming arrival made him anxious.

"There!" cried the second of his three men, his word a puff of hot air pierced by snowfall.

A light bobbed in the distance.

"Why would they travel in this?" asked his third man, the only other to stand with him on the surface. The rest of his lieutenants were in the mine, directing the overseers, who commanded the slaves with lash and rod. "What can be so urgent—"

"Remember," said Rastagar, "obsequious."

Rastagar was confused by the indistinct shape that approached at a dreadfully slow pace. Its true form was obscured by snowfall and the advancing darkness of night. As it drew nearer he saw that it was a fur-wrapped, hulking, bipedal figure. He could discern little else. It held a torch in one hand and wore a harness—pulling a sled with two occupants.

Rastagar and his top lieutenants were silent as the hulking figure pulled the sled to a stop before them. It reached up and yanked down the scarf that was shielding its face from the snow and cold. She was a half-orc.

She dropped the torch in the snow. It did not go out but began to cough and spit, melting a divot. She yanked her fur mittens free and dropped those too. They were tied to her coat and swung as she began to undo the harness, snarling at the frost-stiffened leather and ice-cold buckles.

One of the two passengers leapt from the sled. He advanced, his feet plunging into the snow, to stand before Rastagar and his trio of lieutenants.

"Rastagar," he said, speaking from behind his porcelain mask. He spoke as if the volume of his voice must overcome the roar of the wind, but there was no wind.

"At your service, m'lord." Rastagar struggled with the words. It was one of the few times in his life he had attempted to be obsequious. He was a large man, tall and broad. Such men hate to defer to smaller men, but the hierarchy of the Masks is inviolate.

The Mask reached into his fur coat and produced a folded packet laden with wax seals and ribbons. "By order of Razmir." He thrust the papers at Rastagar. "I am to take over the operation of the mine, temporarily, and to direct digging according to the will of our god."

Rastagar stared at the packet. He looked into the eyes of the other Mask. He found it hard to keep the man's malevolent gaze. He felt other eyes on him and looked. It was the second passenger, watching him. He was bundled in furs and to Rastagar he was like an infant swaddled against the cold. All Rastagar could see of him was a strip of dark skin above his scarf and his eyes, violet eyes that glowed like a fox's.

The higher ranking Mask stepped onto the elevator platform. Rastagar glanced at him then turned and watched as the half-orc, now free of her harness, walked to the side of the sled, bent, and scooped up the seated figure. She held him in one arm, which made him still more like a babe in Rastagar's mind, while she picked up and slid onto her shoulder four leather bags, filled to bursting with supplies. She turned and walked past Rastagar and his men to stand on the platform.

"Down!" snapped the Mask.

. . .

"Review the directives carefully," said the Mask. "Let there be no doubts." He, Rastagar, the female half-orc, and the second man (still wrapped in furs), occupied Rastagar's cramped cabin.

The cabin was at the bottom of the ravine, midway between the elevator and the entrance to the mine. A massive pyramid of timbers loomed over the cabin, timbers used to support the shafts. Rastagar's lieutenants had been dismissed by the Mask. That irritated him, but he kept silent. He set a few split logs on the fire and turned to his superior.

"The mine is not as safe—" began Rastagar, but the malevolent gaze of the Mask silenced him. He found his courage and continued. "We've dug deep as of late." Rastagar glanced at the Mask. "Cut into the Darklands."

"That is immaterial," growled the Mask.

"But the danger—"

"I will not tolerate insubordination."

Rastagar went to the wax-sealed packet. He had set it on the table by his arm-chair. "No," he said, touching the seals but not breaking them. "Of course not. I'm certain everything's in order."

"Then I shall begin at once," said the Mask. He pulled on his fur coat and went to the door. "Your assistance will not be necessary," he said over his shoulder, narrowing his eyes at Rastagar as he spoke. He yanked open the door and stepped out into the snowfall, shutting the door behind him with a *whoosh* that brought cold into the room.

Rastagar collapsed into his arm-chair. His eyes fell on the fur wrapped figure. He watched, half in a daze—for his thinking had been upset—as the slender figure began to divest itself of layers. Rastagar's eyes widened when he beheld a dark elf.

"Not many of my kind in Razmir's priesthood?" The dark elf laughed. "Then again, who knows, since you all wear masks." He unwrapped his legs and studied the look in Rastagar's eyes. "A cripple," he said, patting his legs, which were little more than stunted, gnarled sticks. "Since birth."

He studied his own crippled legs. "My people are in the habit of destroying any offspring born with an obvious deformity." He looked up at Rastagar. "It's a mercy, for dark elf culture does not reward weakness. How did I escape such a fate?" He shrugged his shoulders. "Foolish parents. They got me to the surface. An orphan, hand-delivered to the nearest homestead. I would say that I ran away as soon as I was able, but—"

Both the dark elf and Rastagar heard the collapse of a pile of dirty dishes and looked. The half-orc was searching for a mug, intent on making hot chocolate. She had already found a kettle and a tin of cocoa.

"You can take that off," said the dark elf. Rastagar turned to him. The dark elf nodded, motioning to his mask. "You're in the comfort of your own home. No need to keep it on. Besides, I've seen plenty of Masks without their masks."

Rastagar was hesitant. It was unheard of to remove one's mask before strangers or even before non-Masks one knew, but it remained cold against his face, was uncomfortable at all times, and the dark elf was right, he was in his own home and it seemed silly to think he would wear it always, even in sleep. He reached up, pushing the mask, and lifted it from his head. He set it down on the table next to the ribboned packet.

"I wondered what you looked like," said the dark elf. "I imagined your build, your face."

Rastagar turned to the dark elf. "Who are you?"

"Oh, yes, we haven't been introduced." He motioned to the door. "He's lacking in refinement. Single-minded, one might say." He held out his hand. "Azreth."

Rastagar realized that the dark elf, who had been deposited by the half-orc on the floor near the hearth, could not come to him so he rose, stepped to the seated man, bent, and shook his hand. It was smaller and more delicate than his own. He searched his memory, asking himself if he had ever met a dark elf. He hadn't.

"No doubt," said Azreth, speaking to Rastagar's back as he returned to his chair. "You're wondering why I'm here." He smiled, but his smile faded. "I hate the cold. It's been a miserable day." He glanced at the fire. "And this is making me sleepy." He looked at Rastagar. "You're exhausted. I can see it in your face. It's stress, the stress of having a superior here. I'm right, aren't I?"

The half-orc set the kettle on a hook over the fire and stood close, massaging her breasts through her cotton shirt, for the harness had bruised them. The dark elf looked up at her. He looked at Rastagar. "Allow me a good night's sleep. Tomorrow I'll tell you my tale." He slid himself a bit away from the fire and began to lay out his furs, which were now dry. He scooted himself onto his makeshift bed, lay on his back, and closed his eyes.

Rastagar looked at the half-orc, who had yet to speak a word. She was pouring hot water into *his* favorite mug. Rastagar wondered where she was planning to sleep. His bed was his alone. He didn't imagine she would attempt to squeeze in next to him. The dark elf was so frail he couldn't imagine her lying next to him, either. If she rolled over she would crush him. He shook his head, dismissing his curiosity. He undressed and climbed into bed, lying with his eyes open, watching shadows play on the ceiling above.

"Rastagar?" called Azreth.

Rastagar sat up.

The dark elf motioned to the half-orc, who was settling into Rastagar's arm-chair, her legs extended toward the fire.

"She snarls in her sleep. Don't let it frighten you."

. . .

One of Rastagar's lieutenants pointed but remained mute. He didn't want the Mask to hear him —as he'd already been scolded several times that morning and he hadn't even had breakfast. Rastagar followed the silent directions and found his superior a bit further down the shaft.

"As you can see," said Rastagar, stepping up behind the Mask, who turned and glared at him. Rastagar ignored the dismissive look, after all, it was *his* mine. "Our god's enemies are worked without mercy." The crack of an overseer's whip accentuated his point. "I try to keep them alive as long as possible," said Rastagar, with obvious pride. "They deserve to suffer for their crimes. What I do here is administer justice. I consider it my duty to—"

"What crimes?" snapped the Mask.

Rastagar was a bit taken aback. "Heresy."

"Humph!" The Mask turned his back to Rastagar and consulted a large sheet of parchment. Rastagar looked over the smaller man's shoulder. The parchment was a map. The Mask turned his head and looked up at Rastagar. He folded the map and walked off. Rastagar followed.

"I tried to tell you last night—we've cut into the Darklands."

"Yes, I heard you."

"Things—monsters—have come up. I've lost five guards. Five from fifty is—"

The Mask glanced over his shoulder. "Have you requested more personnel?"

"Um, no, not yet. We filled the tunnel with rubble. That's holding them off for now."

"Then why are you complaining?"

"I'm not—complaining. I'm trying to warn you of the—"

"The danger?" The Mask stopped abruptly and turned. "You've done so twice now, two more times than was necessary. Do you require anything else?"

"Do I— I mean— Do *you* require—"

"You've reviewed the documents by now, yes? I am in charge. I require nothing, not even your presence in the mine. Point of fact, your presence is a hindrance. Your men are used to deferring to you but for the time being they must obey me. Therefore," he jammed his finger into Rastagar's chest. "Your presence in the mine will only confuse them. Go keep an eye on the dark elf." He spun.

"Who *is* he? Why—"

The Mask turned a corner and disappeared from sight.

. . .

"Ever been to Thronestep?" asked Azreth as soon as Rastagar returned to the cabin. Rastagar paused and looked at the dark elf, who was seated on his furs, his back against the wall, his gnarled legs extended before the hearth.

The half-orc was digging through Rastagar's cabinets and trunks, searching for what he had no clue. He would have questioned her, or even scolded her, but he was too intimidated by her powerful physique and her unfriendly demeanor to attempt it.

"Food," said Azreth. "She's looking for food." He glanced at the half-orc. "She eats constantly. Must be all those muscles. She doesn't want to lose them."

The half-orc found a box containing smoked venison, pried the lid free, and sniffed. She took the box to the corner nearest the door, sat crosslegged, and began to sort through the chunks.

"The capital of Razmir? Thronestep?"

Rastagar removed his mask and set it on the table by his arm-chair. The sight of the as-of-yet-unread packet caused him to frown. He smoothed his hair then sat and looked at Azreth. "A few times."

"You know about the Choosing, right?"

Rastagar nodded. He closed his eyes, rest his head back, and rubbed his temples with his fingertips.

"That's why I went," said Azreth. "I figured if I could talk to Razmir, you know, be one of the five chosen for a personal audience, I could beg him to fix these." He patted his crippled legs. "I got tired of waiting." He chuckled. "They say you make your own luck, so—" He shrugged his shoulders, although Rastagar didn't see.

Rastagar opened his eyes and looked at the dark elf, wondering if he was going to talk all day.

"It's an interesting city. The Steps neighborhood is—" Azreth whistled and nodded his head. "As to the Stones," he held out his hands. "It's a lot like a dark elf city, a wide gulf between the haves and the have nots. You know, it's a bit strange how in the statues and architectural flourishes they always have Razmir's mask showing different expressions; martial valor, regal care, divine aloofness. I mean, it's a mask, right? So how can—"

"I guess," said Rastagar, "it's symbolic."

Azreth raised an eyebrow. "Well, well, quite the thinking man, aren't we?" He studied Rastagar. "You know, there's more to you than your brawny exterior hints."

Rastagar wasn't sure how to respond so he didn't. A few moments of silence persisted, in which the half-orc chewed.

"As I said, one makes his own luck. If I wasn't likely to be chosen I figured I'd better find a way to meet Razmir, that is, to gain an audience with a living god. Not easy, to be sure, but there had to be a way."

The half-orc rose, tossing the wooden box into the corner, and went in search of more food.

"Didn't you bring—" began Rastagar, watching her.

"Our own food?" asked Azreth. "Of course." He looked at the half-orc. "She's already eaten her portion and half of mine." He looked at Rastagar and smiled. "What can you do? As I was saying, there had to be a way. I asked myself, what does a living god need. You might think, well, nothing, obviously. That was my first thought as well, but I'm persistent. I started asking around, doing research, you know, getting the cant. That's how I learned about you."

"Me? But what do I have to do with our god? I'm just—"

"Just a priest doing his duty?"

"Yes," said Rastagar. He rose and went to the door. "And now this other Mask comes and—" He caught himself and looked over his shoulder at the dark elf, who was studying him.

"And what?"

"And I shall *continue* to do my duty," said Rastagar, returning to his chair.

"Yes," Azreth smiled, "we all have our part to play."

Rastagar glanced at the door. "Do you know—" He silenced himself, frowning.

"Do I know what he's looking for?"

"Yes!" said Rastagar leaning forward. "I've received new directives from Razmir many times. He commands me to dig new shafts according to his specifications and each time I've done exactly as he's asked. He can rely on me." Rastagar sat back. "Why send—" Again he self-censored, unsure how much of his frustration he could reveal to the dark elf.

"Yes, I know what he's looking for."

Rastagar looked at Azreth.

"I'm the reason he's looking for it, well, sort of. I was just getting to that." He was interrupted by the half-orc, who came at him with a knife. He looked at her. She dropped a handful of yams and onions in his lap and pointed with the knife to the cast iron pot set on the edge of the hearth.

"Stew," she growled.

Azreth took the knife from her and picked up a yam.

"In my investigations I learned that Razmir would send you directions for new shafts. I heard also that you were digging deeper and deeper. As you said yourself, you've gone so deep as to reach the Darklands—my ancestral home." He dropped a handful of diced yams into the pot. The half-orc walked over and poured a pitcher of water into the pot then went in search of more ingredients.

"I got curious. Why would a living god send directions for the sinking of mine shafts? Why send more than one set of directives? I mean, if he's looking for something shouldn't he know where it is? He's a god, after all."

Rastagar detected a hint of heresy and was about to speak but Azreth waved his concern away and continued, now dicing an onion. He glanced at Rastagar. "There's a lot more to the Darklands than anyone on the surface would ever imagine. They aren't just natural caves and underground rivers. Oh no," he shook his head, "there's a lot more than that." He dumped the onion into the pot. "What else?"

The half-orc returned to him with her hands cupped, knelt, and dropped everything she'd found in his lap.

"Well," said Azreth. "It's going to be one odd stew but," he looked up at the half-orc, who was grinning with pride at her assorted finds, "at least you'll be happy."

"Stew," repeated the half-orc. She went to Rastagar and scowled at him. He got the impression she wanted to sit in *his* chair. He resisted at first but imagined her picking him up and holding him like a babe. He thought it possible. He rose and went to his bed, sitting on the edge. The half-orc plopped into his chair—the wood groaning—extended her legs, crossed her arms over her breasts, closed her eyes, and fell asleep.

Azreth busied himself with food prep, humming a little tune to himself. Rastagar rose and went to the arm-chair table, picked up the sealed, ribboned packet and returned to his bed. He broke the seals, untied the ribbons, and unfolded the letter. He read each page, then read them again. He looked up and saw that Azreth had paused his slicing and dicing and was watching him. Rastagar set the letter aside.

"It doesn't say."

Azreth tilted his head.

"It doesn't say what he's looking for," said Rastagar.

Azreth looked down and continued cutting the assorted vegetables. "Of course not." He glanced at

Rastagar. "But I know what he's after." He glanced into the pot and resumed his humming.

. . .

The stew simmered. The half-orc snarled, snored, and growled in her sleep. The cabin filled with the aroma of cooking vegetables. Rastagar ran recent events through his mind, replaying every word. Something, he decided, wasn't right.

He rose, his bed creaking. The half-orc opened her eyes and looked at him. Azreth, who was tending the stew, turned. Rastagar went to the arm-chair table and picked up his mask. He put it on and went to the door.

"The stew's almost ready," said Azreth. "I've got bread in my bag. Aren't you hungry?"

Rastagar paused, his hand on the door handle. He looked over his shoulder. He was about to open the door when the half-orc stood.

"Where are you going?" It was the most she'd said in two days. "You've been ordered to stay out of the mine."

Rastagar studied her face. He was surprised to hear her speak in complete sentences. It was out of character. He looked at Azreth and saw that the dark elf was staring at him, his jaw tense.

"Fresh air," said Rastagar. The half-orc started toward him. Azreth coughed. The half-orc paused. Rastagar pulled open the door and stepped out into the brisk, morning air.

'No,' he thought, 'something's not right. The papers *look* official.' He sighed. The higher ranking Mask was everything he knew them to be: arrogant, condescending, impatient. He shook his head. What didn't make sense was the dark elf and the half-orc. Also, he was bothered by being exiled from the mine. If the Mask was searching for something wouldn't he want Rastagar's help? After all, he knew the mine better than anyone else. Not only that, he had proven his loyalty time and time again.

He went in search of one of his lieutenants, looking in the tool shed and amongst the other buildings and structures on the surface. He glanced at his cabin and saw that the door was open, the half-orc standing just inside, peering out. He turned away. He saw a guard and went over to him, glancing over his shoulder to see if the half-orc could have seen the guard from her vantage point. She couldn't have, as the pyramid of support beams was in the way.

"You there," called Rastagar. The guard, who had not expected to see his boss, snapped to attention. Rastagar stepped close. "I need you to do something for me. I need you to ride to Thronestep."

"Sir?"

"Take another guard with you." Rastagar thought for a moment. "I want you to verify that the Mask that arrived last night is really from Thronestep. I don't know what's going on, but something's not right. Go now, and ride hard."

"Yes, Sir."

. . .

Fridolin, a mercenary, one of a dozen forming a loose cordon around the Forgotten Track (mercenary being an uncommon occupation for a halfling), lifted the spyglass to his right eye, closing the left. 'Two horsemen?' He glanced at the position of the sun. "Damn you Azreth. How could you have known?"

He watched the two men lead the horses from the elevator platform. They weren't wearing masks. That was good. He watched as the two men rose into the saddles and kicked their horses into a gallop. He collapsed the spyglass and dropped it into one of the pockets of his fur coat. He stepped to the wicker bird cage, removed the heavy cloth covering it—protecting its occupants from the cold—and opened the door. He lifted the cage and shook it. A dozen blackbirds darted through the door. They rose in an uncertain arc, got their bearings, then flew in a cluster to the east.

Fridolin dropped the cage, took out his spyglass, and telescoped it. He scanned the road going south until he saw movement. The camouflage was cast aside and a half-dozen men ran—having seen the blackbirds—toward the road. Fridolin turned and scanned the road until he spotted the two horsemen from the mine. "Hurry, they're riding fast. Rastagar must have put the fear of Razmir into them."

He turned the spyglass back toward the ambush spot. He could no longer see his fellow mercenaries. He looked back at the two horsemen, tracking their furious ride. The lead horse slid to a stop and reared up, the rider nearly thrown from the saddle. A net had risen up between a pair of trees on either side of the road. The second horseman was just able to stop in time.

Fridolin watched as his companions emerged from behind the leafless bushes and the trees supporting the rope net, lifting their heavy crossbows. The two men tried for their swords but numerous bolts slammed into them before they could mount a defense or turn away.

The first horseman slumped forward then fell to the side, disappearing for a moment behind the obstacle of the horse, only to reappear as a crumpled mass in the blood-stained snow.

The second horseman too fell, onto his butt. He tried to scoot away, only one of his legs kicking up snow and gravel, the other pierced by two bolts—paralyzed by pain. He was trying to draw his sword when a bolt struck him in the chest and he lay still.

Fridolin watched as his fellow mercenaries grabbed the reins, leading the horses from the road, as they took down the net, and as they cleared the corpses and kicked snow over the blood.

"War is the 'fair cloth wov'n of men," he said as he collapsed his spyglass. "And blood is sword-drink."[1]

. . .

---

[1] From *The Mirror and the Mask* by Jorge Luis Borges; although, I think Borges is quoting someone else—Shakespeare? or perhaps one of the Icelandic sagas.

Razmir studied one of his slaves. There were two in the room, his scrying room. He was close to her, close enough she would have felt his breath against her lips, if he wasn't wearing his mask. He was evaluating the stitches that kept her eyes closed, kept her from seeing him.

She knew he was standing before her. She could feel his presence. She tried not to tremble, for she feared him. Not many of his slaves served long. She wore a simple dress of white cotton with gold trim. She was nude beneath. She was barefoot and wore no jewelry. Her luxurious black hair—which had been a pride to her—had been shaved and she was bald-headed. She felt his attention turn away, but her nervous tremble did not lessen.

Razmir studied the stitches on his male slave's eyes. Like the other, his head had been shaved. He wore a waist wrap of white cotton also with gold trim. He was barefoot and bare-chested. The flesh around his eyes, through which the thick, wax-coated thread had been stitched, was red and puffy. Razmir was satisfied. He knew neither of their names and did not care to. All that mattered was that they serve him and never see him.

He lifted the enchanted, golden mask from his face and flung it toward the nearest sofa. It bounced and settled face-down. He pulled free his black leather gloves and tossed those, only one landing on the sofa, the other on the floor. He rubbed the palm of his left hand over his bald pate and sighed. He went to the mirror and gazed into it, sighing still more heavily.

"Pour it," he growled.

The female slave, her name was Bianca, although Razmir would never know, turned and began forward. Her thighs banged into the stone lip of the scrying pool. She felt out with one hand, gauging the depth of the pool. She judged it to be only a half-inch deep and guessed that the stone dish must be on a support of some kind. She positioned the pitcher and poured.

"You," growled Razmir. "Add your blood." He was speaking to the male slave, whose name was Uys, yet another name which the living god would never know.

Uys turned and felt his way forward. They had been shown the room before their eyes were sewn shut and expected to memorize its layout. In their terrified state neither could retain a perfect recall. Uys bumped into Bianca, whispered an apology, then felt around her until he found the scrying pool. Razmir watched him stumbling in his reflection in the mirror.

Uys paused, his arms dropping to his side. "Master," he said, his voice trembling. "I've no knife."

Razmir scoffed. "Did I not give you teeth?"

"Yes, Master," said Uys. He raised his hand to his mouth, bit into his palm, and squeezed his blood into the pool.

"Kneel."

Bianca and Uys did as they were commanded.

Razmir went to the scrying pool and began the long litany of a spell.

. . .

The trio of wizards sat around the smokeless, soundless fire, which was the result of a spell. Lotte was Taldan, from Molthune, short and plump, with curly reddish-blonde hair and ruddy cheeks. Her eyes were blue. Her face had a spattering of freckles. Her fingers, which were for the moment hidden beneath fur mittens, held multiple rings, all of which she'd crafted and enchanted herself.

Caspar was thin and bald despite his youth. His hairlessness, which applied to all of him, even his eyelashes, was the result of a magical experiment gone awry. He was exceedingly odd in personality. It was a trial of patience to speak to him. Unlike Lotte, who wore furs, he wore only a tight-fitting body suit of black leather. He did not shiver, despite the thinness of his leathers or the fact his bald head was exposed. He seemed inured to the cold. Or perhaps, because he worshipped Zon-Kuthon, the god of suffering, he was enjoying the sensation of freezing to death.

The leader of the trio was Jeroen, a black-haired elf, angular of features, imperious of demeanor, who wore a haughty expression, this being one of only three moods he seemed capable of. The other two being the dismissal of a lesser intellect and shock that someone would say or do something so stupid in his presence.

They were not sitting idly, but were concentrating. Nearby the two horses taken from the dead guards kicked at the snow and earth, hoping to reveal something edible. A cluster of mercenaries huddled as near as they could get to the fire without annoying the wizards. They were curled up on their bedrolls, their furs pulled up to their eyes. Only the three wizards had a fire. No normal fire could be made for fear of the smoke being seen. The trio had laughed off a suggestion they produce multiple fires so others could be warmed.

Lotte opened her eyes. "He's beginning. I can feel him."

"Yes," hissed Caspar. "His shadow races toward us."

"Begin the illusion," said Jeroen. "Keep your timing by my words. If we do not work together—" But the magic of Razmir's spell washed over them like the light of a flaming meteor passing overhead. All three fell into a synchronized chant.

. . .

Razmir gazed into the blood-tinted water of the scrying pool. He watched as a bird's-eye view of the Forgotten Track materialized. He saw the expanse of snow, the leafless branches of the trees and the complicated shadows they cast. He saw the deep cut of the ravine. He mentally zoomed in and saw the wood beams of the elevator and the taunt rope as thick as a man's arm. He directed his attention over the edge. He had the experience of one falling headlong. Even though he'd done that a dozen times his heart still leapt.

He raced past Rastagar's cabin. The windows were dark. No smoke rose from the chimney. He dove through the mine's entrance. For a moment the scrying pool was as black as ink. The light of lanterns materialized. He dove downwards again, past the elevator that led deeper into the mine. He raced past his prisoners, past their overseers—ducking under their whips. He curled past Rastagar's lieutenants. He had the childish thought to reach out and knock off their masks. Of course, because he was only seeing them via divination magic and not actually present, he could not follow up on his impulse.

Razmir was as familiar with the penal colony/mine as Rastagar, perhaps more-so, as he was more intelligent than his obedient priest and had a far better memory. He found the most recent tunnel to cut into the Darklands. It was filled with rubble. He backed up and went down other tunnels, finding little gaps and openings through which one got a view of massive caverns lit up by glowing lichen or of drops of hundreds of feet into lightless voids. He was amused at the thought of a prisoner breaking through to such a free fall.

He searched the tunnels until he found Rastagar. He observed him for a moment, watching the large man squeeze uncomfortably into the low-ceiling space. He had no sympathy for his worshipper's discomfort. He only wanted him to work harder, to drive the prisoners harder, to find what he was looking for—before it was too late.

Satisfied that all was well he began to back out of the mine, moving in reverse. He could have ended the spell but he enjoyed the sensation of moving backwards, as if he was rewinding time itself, the act of a true god.

He swore he saw a Mask that should not have been there. One that was too highly ranked to be in the mine. He paused and looked but saw only a slave hunched over a rock, banging pathetically at it with a pickax.

"Hmmm." Razmir reached out and gripped the top of Uys's head. He began to knead his slave's scalp like one kneads dough. He swore he saw a Mask but now he could not find him. He turned his gaze left and right, but saw only the prisoners and their overseers. He had the worry of a creeping senility, grew angry at the thought, released Uys's scalp, and dismissed his spell with a growl.

. . .

Lotte turned to the side and vomited.

Caspar's eyes rolled up and he fainted, falling backwards to land with a *poof* in the snow.

Jeroen realized his whole body was tense. He had balled his fists so tightly his nails had cut into his palms. He forced himself to relax, then wiped the sweat from his brow. "It worked!"

"Barely!" said Lotte. She stood and spit. She pointed an accusing finger at Jeroen. "If he would have pressed harder—"

Jeroen stood and pointed back. "But he did *not*!"

"You were a fool to sign onto this job!" said Lotte. "We could all be dead!"

Jeroen was about to argue but he smiled instead. He looked at Caspar. "Better check and see that he isn't."

. . .

Rastagar woke before dawn and prayed to Razmir, as was his habit. He felt as if someone were watching him or eavesdropping but Azreth appeared to be asleep and the half-orc was snoring. After his morning devotions he had the thought to go to the mine but instead he sat on the edge of his bed and brooded.

. . .

Azreth was shaken awake—a dagger at his throat.

"Who are you? Why are you here?"

"Easy, Rastagar." Azreth reached up and placed his hand on Rastagar's wrist, but did not try to force the dagger away. "Keep your voice down. Whatever you do, don't wake her. She'll kill us both."

This was not the response Rastagar expected. He glanced over his shoulder at the half-orc, who was slumped in his arm-chair, her head back, mouth open. He turned back to Azreth.

"Tell me what's going on or *I'll* kill *you* both."

"I told him this wasn't the way to do it," said Azreth. "I told him not to hide it from you."

"What are you talking about? Who did you—"

"Rastagar, please, it's hard to stay calm when you're holding a dagger to a man's throat. You'll be yelling soon. Put it away and sit close. I'll tell you everything. But if either of us wakes her, we're dead."

Rastagar hesitated but after a struggle with his emotions his reason won and he set the dagger aside. He sat next to Azreth, facing the slumbering half-orc. Azreth sat up and scooted so that his back was against the hearth. He was facing Rastagar, his crippled legs turned awkwardly to the side.

"I lied to you." There was just enough dawn light filtering through the windows for Azreth to look into Rastagar's eyes. "I had to." He glanced at the half-orc. "You might assume she's my assistant, to move me about. Or you might have assumed she's his assistant, the other Mask." He shook his head. "She's my jailer, in a sense, and may be my executioner." He looked at Rastagar. "I didn't seek out Razmir. Sure, I went to the Choosing, more out of curiosity than hope. I think that's when they became aware of me, the Masks. I was taken that night. They killed my man, a servant—a friend, really—who helped me get around." Azreth paused, frowning.

"I was interrogated—tortured. There was a Mask there who was *different*. His mask was made out of gold, not glazed porcelain like all the others. I could feel arcane might oozing off of him. He was directing the questioning. They asked me about the Darklands. They were already familiar with quite a lot, more than any other surface dwellers I've ever met. They asked about Nar-Voth, Orv, and the Vault Keepers.

"I know those words mean nothing to you and they aren't important at this moment. They questioned me all night. Their questions were leading somewhere. Yet, they were being secretive. It was obvious they wanted me to divulge certain information without them having to ask for it. I didn't know what they wanted so I told them everything I could think of."

The half-orc snorted, choked on her own spit, and sat up. She coughed several times then turned and spit on the floor. She growled a curse under her breath, turned in the chair, tucked her head into the crook of her arm, and went back to sleep. Both Azreth and Rastagar were silent for a few minutes until she began snarling and snoring.

"He dismissed them," continued Azreth. "They tried to protest, saying it was too dangerous to be left alone with me. He laughed. I would have laughed too, but— They left, even the bastard who'd been hitting me. It was just me and," Azreth looked at Rastagar, "Razmir."

"Razmir?"

Azreth nodded. "He asked me what he wanted to ask me. He even told me why he asked. He didn't need to, it was obvious why he wanted what he wanted as soon as I knew what it was." Azreth sighed. "Forgive my obtuseness. I'm afraid to speak about what he said. He might hear me, as silly as that sounds."

"You spoke with—a god?"

"A— I've been crippled all my life. I know what it's like to have your body betray you. I know what it's like to have every movement, every action—the things others do without a thought—be a difficulty and a source of pain. I can see this pain in others." He studied Rastagar's face. "Have you ever asked yourself, why does he wear a mask?"

Rastagar, who had been watching the half-orc for clues of wakefulness, turned to Azreth. "Why does he— His face—to look upon a god's face—" He shook his head. "It would blind you, drive you mad, probably kill you. He wears a mask to protect us, those who worship him. He wears a mask because he loves us."

"Have you seen him walk?"

"What?"

"Have you seen him sit down or stand up?"

"I—" Rastagar shook his head. "I've never been that close."

"Rastagar, I'm going to tell you something and you're going to want to scream and yell and hit me but I beg you, don't. You may think she's just a savage, just some brute who you might be able to kill with your dagger. I'm telling you she's much more. If you value your life, hold your tongue." Azreth evaluated the emotions behind Rastagar's expression before continuing. "He's an old man and he's getting older."

Rastagar's eyes went wide. His mouth dropped open.

"His knees are bad and his back aches."

Rastagar stood, his fists balled, his entire body shaking.

"He wears a mask because he doesn't want anyone to see that he's aging."

Rastagar unclenched his fist, bent, and backhanded Azreth. "You blasphemy!"

Azreth looked at the half-orc. He did not cry out or even move to staunch the flow of blood that ran from his busted lip. Azreth's serious demeanor paused Rastagar's anger. He looked at the half-orc. She was brought out of her deep slumber by his shout but she was not fully awake. She stretched her legs, repositioned her head, and slumped back into a deep sleep.

"What he's after is called Ilvarandin." Azreth looked up at Rastagar. "What do you think those directions are for? You've been looking for Ilvarandin for years and you didn't even know it."

"Ilvarandin?" Rastagar sat back down.

"I don't know much about it," said Azreth, pressing his sleeve to his lip. "Rumors. Maybe it was made by the Vault Keepers. Maybe by someone else. I don't think Razmir cares who made it. All he cares about is what it promises—immortality. That's what he's looking for, Rastagar. The fountain of youth. The wellspring of life. What Razmir wants—what he needs—is to reverse the aging process, to be young again and to never grow old. That's why this mine exists. That's why you dig." Azreth shook his head. "Not because you're punishing heretics."

"But I— My duty— My obedience— My faith —"

"I heard you praying. Has he ever answered your prayers?"

Rastagar rose and staggered away from Azreth, who watched him with his fox-like eyes. He spun, avoiding the half-orc's outstretched legs, grabbed his mask and his cloak, and went to the door. He yanked it open and half-ran, half-fell out into the frigid air. He threw his cloak around his shoulders and stumbled across the pristine white expanse, his feet breaking through the crust of ice on top of the snow.

Rastagar fitted his mask and entered the mine. A slave was crouched just inside the opening, pressed against the stone wall, trying to shield himself from the cold. There was no door or other barricade which might offer shelter.

The slave looked up at Rastagar but he was so concerned with his own misery—he wore only rags, his feet wrapped in thin strips of worn cloth—he didn't comprehend the misery that the Mask now standing over him could bring.

It was the slave's unwanted job to operate the elevator that led deeper into the mine. He was chained to the wench. When the slave did not rise and grasp the lever, Rastagar had the notion to strike the man, he even lifted his hand to do so, but something stopped him. He studied the man shivering in the morning gloom. A man, just like him. Cold, just like him. The slave, coming to his senses upon seeing the raised fist, stood and grabbed the lever at last. He lowered his eyes but watched Rastagar, preparing to either dodge or do his duty.

Rastagar took off his cloak, stepped toward the slave, and wrapped it around his shoulders. He tried to say that he would see to having the chain removed but the words didn't come out, only a few mumbled syllables. He found he could not look into the other man's eyes. He stepped onto the platform and waited, looking down. The slave pulled the lever. The wench started and Rastagar began his descent.

. . .

'All my life,' thought Rastagar, 'I've served Razmir. I have faith in him—a living god.' He shook his head, as if to fling free the doubts that Azreth had sown. 'I believe in doing my duty. I believe in obedience to a higher power—to Razmir. I believe in justice.' He thought of all he'd given up in order to adhere to his beliefs.

He had never married. He suffered loneliness. Despite his vigor he had not enjoyed the love of a woman in years—so long that he could not recall his last tender embrace. He had given up the striving for wealth and fame. Neither could come to him in the Forgotten Track. Oh, yes, he realized, there was silver, gold, and even precious stones freed from the rock but none of it was his. It all went to Thronestep, to his god. And yes, he thought, 'Razmir knows that I serve him faithfully. He's always known.'

That thought, that his good works were known to Razmir, that he occupied precious territory in the mind of a living god, had always sustained him. If he had given up a mortal reward so be it, he would be rewarded in the afterlife—the true reward. But the value of that proposition was crumbling. *Have you seen him walk? Have you seen him sit down or stand up?* These words echoed in his mind. How, he wondered, could a god with bad knees and an aching back reward him in the afterlife? *Has he ever answered your prayers?*

Rastagar began to tremble. His entire life took on a new frame. The mine, the directives to dig here or there—groping like a hand in darkness. Rastagar never questioned *why*. He did as he was told. He tasked his lieutenants, they commanded the overseers, and the whips forced the slaves to work. He had always told himself it was justice. Those men and women—and even children—who struggled to lift their master's tools, who were malnourished, fatigued, beaten, and forever hovering near death's door, deserved their cruel fates because they were heretics. All that mattered to Rastagar was that justice was done. A living god had been blasphemed against —his love betrayed—and it was his duty to see that punishment was meted out.

What he's after is called Ilvarandin.... That's why this mine exists. That's why you dig.

"But a living god doesn't *need*," whispered Rastagar.

The elevator creaked to a halt. A guard slid open the door and saluted. Rastagar grabbed the man's tunic and yanked him close. The guard looked at him, eyes wide, mouth agape.

"There's a slave," Rastagar motioned with his head upwards, indicating the slave to whom he had given his cloak. "Remove his chains." Rastagar stepped from the elevator and flung the guard into the car.

"But I—"

"Go to the tool shed and find a pry bar."

"Sir?"

"Free him," said Rastagar. "Then leave."

"Leave?"

"Leave this place."

Rastagar stepped to the side and slammed the lever back. The wench reversed itself and with a jerk the car began the return. The guard slid the door shut, watching his boss through the gap.

Rastagar spun. He felt his mask slip and paused. He grabbed it and yanked it free. He turned it in his hands and looked at it. *Is this how others see me? What can they know of me, hidden behind this—thing.* He dropped the mask at his feet and stood looking down at it. He knew it was a symbol. He knew that for most of his life the mask that was now at his feet had been the shield of his defense, the banner of his authority, and the club of his power. He stared at it for a long time.

The sounds of the mine: the sharp wrap of iron on stone, the groans of labor, a cascade of pebbles, all came to him—reminding him of where he stood. The mask changed before his eyes. Now he saw it differently. It was a sham, a crutch, a lie, and ultimately it was an excuse. An excuse for cruelty, tyranny, and self-deception.

He turned away and saw a rack on which were several pickaxes. He staggered to the rack and grabbed one. He staggered back to the mask and raised the pickax overhead. For a moment he wavered. He had been a Mask for so long. He believed in Razmir. To destroy his mask was not only an act of self-destruction it was sacrilege. His arms shook. His stomach tightened. His head began to ache. His resolve strengthened. He bent nearly double and drove the tip of the pickax into the mask. It shattered, part of it crumbling from the force of the blow.

Rastagar's knees went weak. He stumbled to the rack and leaned against it. His face grew hot. He began to sweat. His mouth was dry and he longed for a sip of wine. He glanced at the mask. It had lost all of its power and meaning. All he saw was broken pottery. He looked up at the rough stones overhead. "I've destroyed it, Razmir. I've committed a sin against you. Strike me down. Do you hear me? Strike me down!" His voice echoed through the mine and came back to him. He shook his head. "No, you can't, can you? Because you're *not* a god." He rose and went to the pickax. "You're just an old man."

He pulled the pickax free and began to hunt for the other Mask.

"Where is he?" Rastagar yelled when he saw one of his lieutenants. The man, who was wearing his mask, turned and stared at Rastagar. He was stunned to see his naked face.

"Is everything— Are you—"

Rastagar grabbed his shirt and pulled him close. He released his shirt and grabbed his mask. He yanked it free and threw it at his feet. He lifted the pickax and dropped it on the mask. It crumbled beneath the heavy steel head. His lieutenant was shocked and could do nothing but stare in disbelief. "The mine is closed," growled Rastagar. "Get everyone out."

"My mask!" His lieutenant looked up from the crumbled remains. "The mine—"

"They're free. They're all free." Rastagar once more grabbed his lieutenant's shirtfront. "Do you hear me?"

"But, I—"

Rastagar flung the man aside and lifted the pickax, growling. His lieutenant scrambled away from him, looking over his shoulder as he fled. Rastagar laughed and continued on. He saw an overseer whipping a woman who had fallen with a load of stones she was carrying in a wicker basket. The overseer was laughing. The woman was screaming.

Rastagar charged the overseer and slammed his shoulder into the man's back, knocking him down. He lifted the pickax and swung it in a violent arc but the overseer rolled to the side. He leapt to his feet and ran away howling. Rastagar helped the woman stand.

She was too stunned to thank him and he was too emotional to speak an apology.

He heard a commotion and spun. Several guards appeared and with them one of his lieutenants.

"Rastagar!" said the masked lieutenant. "What are you—"

"I've one final order to give," said Rastagar. "Empty the mine."

"Empty the mine?"

"It's over. The mine is closed." He looked at the faces of the guards. "You're fired." He turned and looked at a nearby overseer. "If you don't get out, I'll kill you!"

"What are you talking about?" asked his lieutenant. "What's going on?"

"Where is he?"

"Who?" asked his lieutenant.

"The Mask."

His lieutenant turned and looked over his shoulder. He turned back to Rastagar.

"Get out!" screamed Rastagar. "Pray to the gods —the *real* gods—I never see any of you again!" He shouldered the pickax and began down the shaft.

He found the Mask leaning over a table, on which was spread the pages of a drawing illuminated by candles. When he heard movement he looked. When he saw Rastagar he stood erect and turned to face him. Rastagar lifted the pickax. He yelled and charged but the Mask dodged the blow, diving to the side. The point of the pickax became buried in the wooden top of the table. Rastagar pried it free.

"What are you—" He could not complete his question. He had to roll to dodge a second attack. He got his feet under him and crouched. "You've gone insane!"

"No!" screamed Rastagar as he swung the pickax. It was an unwieldy weapon and the Mask was able to slip out of the way. "For the first time in my life I see the truth!"

The Mask rushed a few yards away and turned. "You'll pay for this treachery!"

Rastagar made a half-hearted sweep with the pickax. The Mask turned and ran. Rastagar leaned against the wall, spent. He dropped the pickax and slid down into a seated position, laughing and crying.

. . .

Rastagar sat in his arm-chair. He looked around his cabin. It had been trashed, his meagre possessions overturned and broken. He had to set his chair upright to sit.

Where Azreth and the half-orc had gone he hadn't a clue and he didn't care. He assumed the Mask had fled to the surface, collected them, and departed. He had no love for the dark elf, neither did he wish him harm. He hoped what Azreth had said about the half-orc becoming his executioner wouldn't prove true.

He rose, went to the door and opened it. He looked up and to his left. The last of the slaves were stepping from the elevator platform. The overseers were the first to flee, followed by the guards. It was most likely the guards who had stolen the petty cash.

The slaves, far more numerous, were slow to assemble and leave. Where could they go? Most of them didn't really know where they were, what might be around, or which way was safe. Rastagar had remained in the mine, caught in the turbulence of despair and euphoria, as the slaves searched the buildings above. They took anything that appeared useful, may have value, and could be carried. Mostly, though, they wanted food, water, and clothing.

He turned and looked one last time over the simple one-room cabin that had been his home and his hermitage. It no longer felt like a home. He no longer wanted a hermitage. He stepped out onto the trampled snow and made his way to the elevator. He pulled the lever. The wench began to whirl with a throaty whine. The lowering platform cast a pale shadow over him. He stepped onto the platform and flung the lever. The elevator began its ascent.

'All I ever wanted, all that was important to me, was to do my duty. I wanted to please my god, whom I loved and who I thought loved me.' He felt tears drop onto his bare cheeks. He was struck by the chilly wetness. He had always worn his mask and so his tears, had he shed them, would have been sheltered from the cold. 'But I haven't been loved. There was no justice. I didn't rule, I tyrannized. I wasn't obedient, I was cruel.'

The platform reached the surface and he stepped off. He could see the slaves walking in strung-out clusters, heading away from Thronestep. No doubt they had seen the overseers and guards in the distance, heading toward the city, and had made the obvious choice. He turned to the southwest and imagined he could see the capital on the horizon. For a moment he had the reckless thought to confront Razmir, to go to the Choosing, stand up, and proclaim the truth, but he wasn't suicidal. He turned and followed the slaves, who were now free—same as he.

. . .

Azreth wrapped his right arm around the half-orc's muscular neck. She was holding him like a babe, cradling him in the crux of her left arm. She held out a lantern with the other. He was giddy and as it was just the two of them he gave her a peck on the cheek. She looked at him and smiled.

"He tried to kill me," said the Mask. He came to stand beside Azreth and the half-orc. He was holding his mask—a perfect forgery—in his right hand. "You said you had the most dangerous job."

"I lied," said Azreth.

"I'll remember that when it comes time to divvy up—"

"You didn't have the most dangerous job, either," interrupted Azreth. "Those poor wizards did."

"If we would have failed," called Jeroen. "We'd *all* be dead."

The half-orc turned, so both she and Azreth could see the elven mage. His two partners, Lotte and

Caspar walked up behind him. Behind them came the mercenaries.

"Rastagar?" asked Azreth.

"To the northeast, same as the slaves," said Fridolin.

"The guards?"

"On their way to Thronestep."

"We should hurry," said Jeroen. "He may scry again."

Fridolin smiled and looked up at the taller man. "All you had to do was ask." He passed Azreth and the half-orc, who turned. He went to the vault door and stood examining the trio of locks. "Light, please."

"Allow me," said Lotte. She said a few short, sharp words. A half-dozen glowing balls of light manifest, floating before the vault door.

"The best make," said Fridolin, tapping one of the locks with his fingertip. "Expert craftsmanship."

"Save the suspense," said Azreth. "We're short on time."

Fridolin produced his picks and torsion bar and began to work the locks. It didn't take long. The half-orc set Azreth down at her feet, stepped past him, grabbed the edge of the vault door, and pulled it open —every muscle straining. She backed away as the magical orbs darted within. She picked up Azreth and, now that she too was giddy, kissed his cheek. Everything he had said had been true. Everything he had planned had happened.

"We pulled it off," she whispered.

All stood gazing into the natural cave which had been secured by the heavy iron door and triplicate lock. They were stunned into silence by the open-topped crates filled with silver, electrum, and gold ores. Just inside was a stout wooden chest banded with iron and inside it, they surmised, were precious stones.

"Almost a year's worth," said Azreth. "Come spring this would have been shipped to Thronestep, to be smelted and refined, minted into coins, and spent by Razmir and his lackeys." He looked over the men and women in his employ. "Well, don't stand there gawking." He looked into the vault. "Our loot isn't going to steal itself."

Of Art and Avarice

Old Khalden sat crosslegged on a woven mat at the periphery of the small square, one of many in the gilded city of Oppara, capital of Taldor. He was Kelish, with that race's bronze skin and luxurious black hair; although, his was more white than black. He was blind, having been blinded as a punishment for a crime committed in his passionate youth.

None knew the story. Khalden never spoke of it. When asked, a sentimental mood gathered his features into a wistful sadness and a sigh escaped his lips. No doubt—thought those who saw the old beggar's face at such moments—he had traded his sight for love.

It was assumed that Old Khalden was nothing more than a beggar or perhaps an ascetic, for amongst his few visible possessions was a time-worn copy of the *Order of Numbers,* Abadar's holy book. What use a blind man could make of such a book few could surmise.

Old Khalden was not what he seemed. His begging bowl was never emptied. The coins of silver and copper that filled its shallow depth had done so for years. He seemed to have no need of them. This was because Old Khalden was no beggar at all, but was a member in good standing of the Brotherhood of Silence, one of the most prominent thieves' guilds in the Inner Sea region.

He was retired from active work. He occupied himself with his current duties, that of a overhearer of words spoken, more to make himself feel useful than for any need to impress his betters, for he had already done so. Few could guess that when the blind beggar was not to be found on his mat he was enjoying life's rich bounty, tucked away out of sight in the Brotherhood of Silence's labyrinthine headquarters, one entrance of which, lie not more than a dozen steps from his right hand.

It was night in the gilded city. Few were out-of-doors. The free-standing stalls in the square were covered. Only Desna's glowing orb and an assortment of night-roving birds kept the blind beggar company. Not for long, however. Old Khalden turned an ear to the hidden entrance. The door slid open. To his ear the grating sound was an offense. His hand slipped under the leather cover of the *Order of Numbers*. He fingered the enchanted dagger held within, sheathed, as it were, by the cut-out pages of Abadar's holy script.

"Pissed off Tilly, again" grumbled a youthful male. "Two nights in a row with *you*. I'll make a present to her of those raspberry tarts Mara bakes. Then—" A ruffle of fabric silenced the youth. Old Khalden replaced his palm on Abadar's holy book and resumed his feigned sublime indifference to worldly affairs.

"Why's *he* still awake?" whispered Eshkol. "What company I keep; one blind, the other stupid." He moved opposite the hidden entrance, away from Old Khalden, whose true identity he did not know, the two never having crossed paths in the poorly lit hallways behind the secret entrance. Eshkol found a shadow and squatted on his haunches. His companion, Owen, another young apprentice of the Brotherhood, followed, managed to fit himself into the same shadow, and also squatted. "Dawn can't come soon enough," complained Eshkol. "These watches are pointless. Who's going to sneak in here, anyway?"

"Guards?" asked Owen.

"They don't sneak, fool."

"They—"

"Besides, the only guards that matter are bought off. Do you think the Brotherhood is stupid? You have a lot to—"

"I hear a troubling sound," said Old Khalden, speaking seemingly to himself, but loud enough to be heard by the youths. "It is the voice of ignorance. But how can that be?"

"Shut up, old loon," called Eshkol. Even though he had no fear of the blind beggar he lowered his voice. He elbowed Owen, who lost his balance and fell into the moonlight. He rose, squeezed himself once more into the shadow and squatted. He took no offense at his companion's actions. "You really are useless," said Eshkol. "If they didn't need someone to move around their trunks of loot without emptying them you'd be sitting over there," he pointed to Old Khalden. "How could you fail the first test? The *first* test!"

"They weren't mine."

"That's the entire—Ugh." Eshkol lowered his head into his hands. "They left the gold out to test you," he said, looking at Owen. "If you don't seize every opportunity to take gold when it's right in front of your eyes then how will the Brotherhood know your heart's filled with greed?"

"But," said Owen. "We shouldn't steal from each other, should we?"

"What did Tilly tell you?" asked Eshkol. Tilly was the unfortunate thief who had been placed in charge of the two youth's instruction. "There's no such crime as theft. Remember? There's only the crime of being caught."

"Right," said Owen. "No such crime as—"

"Shut up."

For a few minutes the two young thieves squatted in silence.

"Who's that?" asked Owen, motioning with his head. Eshkol, who had been contemplating how best to rise quickly through the ranks of the Brotherhood of Silence, grabbed his dagger. Owen had a cudgel, owing to his greater strength. Neither youth noticed that Old

Khalden's hand was now beneath the cover of Abadar's holy book.

"Who? Where?"

"There?" motioned Owen. Eshkol looked then looked to his companion.

"Are you—" Eshkol looked back at the "person" Owen had indicated. "That's a statue, are you—" Neither boy noticed that Old Khalden's hand was resting on the book's cover once more.

"A statue?" asked Owen. He narrowed his eyes. "Wasn't there last night."

"No," said Eshkol, "it wasn't. They put it up today. Haven't you noticed them out here working? They spent an entire week clearing—Ugh." He once more placed his head in his hands.

"She's beautiful," said Owen. "Who is she?"

Eshkol looked at Owen, then to the statue. He was about to insult his fellow apprentice again, but the otherworldly presence of the statue gave him pause. The moonlight seemed to animate it. The statue was so expertly crafted that it possessed none of the still-life quality that hobbles the effectiveness of lesser works. Indeed, it appeared so lifelike that Owen could hardly be faulted for mistaking it for a living person.

"How should I—" Began Eshkol.

"Come, young ruffians," said Old Khalden. "You make more noise than a murder of crows." He waved the two youths to him. "In order to silence your ignorant chatter I will tell you what you want to know. Come."

Owen turned to Eshkol.

"Eh, why not?" asked Eshkol.

"We'll get in trouble," said Owen, although when Eshkol rose, he did too.

"We can still see the entrance," whispered Eshkol. "Come on, I'm bored to death."

The pair rose, crossed the square, pausing to gaze at the statue, then arrived at Old Khalden's mat. They studied the blind beggar, looked at each other, then sat, mimicking Khalden's pose, legs folded beneath them.

"All week, I'm listening to the workmen," began Old Khalden. "This morning, when she," he waved his hand toward the statue, whose eyes seemed to have settled on the two youths and their blind instructor, "was placed, a bard came and told her story. Shall I tell you?"

"That's why we're sitting here, old fool," said Eshkol.

Khalden smiled. He patted the cover of the *Order of Numbers,* thinking of its true contents. He remembered how he was in his youth and thought the young thief across from him rather tame. "When the workmen placed the statue," said Old Khalden, "a dwarven man stood in the shadow that you yourselves occupied only moments ago. He was weeping."

"How could you know—" began Eshkol.

Khalden tapped his right ear.

"A dwarf cannot weep quietly," he said, "when they succumb to such emotions, it is with the power of a mountain stream." He organized the telling in his mind. "She was a princess," he said. "One of the many daughters of the previous satrap of Qadira, our old enemy, yes? Now we have peace." He smiled. "And to adhere a man to peace, his heart is secured with love. Or so the bard said." He turned his head toward the statue. He could not see it, but could imagine it. "She was the daughter of man but had something of the djinn about her, that being the genie-folk who flutter upon the wind, lighter than a bird, yet more terrible than a desert twister—should one anger them."

"Old fool, what's this?"

"Go," said Khalden, without anger, "gaze upon her likeness, if you wish to test my telling." The two young thieves rose and went to the statue. They studied it in earnest. The princess, they still did not know her name, was thin to the point of delicateness. Carved into her flesh were swirls and lines meant to represent the straight gusting and whimsical curling of the winds. She had none of the genie-folk's inhuman appearance, being entirely recognizable in form, and of exceptional beauty. The youths returned and sat. Old Khalden continued.

"She was promised to Stavian's Uncle—"

"The Grand Prince?" asked Owen.

"Yes. This Uncle, Hendrik by name, is a most disagreeable man, ugly within and without. He managed to make it to his fiftieth year without once turning the head of a maiden." This made the two youths giggle. "So when he sought a wife one had to be found from amongst the former enemy, a retribution, I suppose.

"The match was entirely inappropriate, of course," continued Khalden. "This princess was shy but watchful. She was like a timid cat, one who is frightened by any sound, yet who is so desiring of petting, she lingers, at war with her own fright. While her betrothed was a man of large appetites, wont to take in-hand immediately any object of his desire. Only the spite of the Grand Prince kept them apart.

"You see, Grand Prince Stavian did not know just how beautiful his Uncle's bride was until he saw her. He postponed the wedding and housed her in the palace. This was so he could gaze upon her. Even though he couldn't or wouldn't marry her, he could still enjoy the sight of her. He is an exceedingly lecherous man.

"The Princess, her name was Fatima, did you know? Ah, well, so it was. She was used to the beauty of her homeland. The city of Katheer, from whence she hails, is home to more wonders than a man could find on his own, even given ten lifetimes in which to search. Even though we cling to our past glory and see its ghost everywhere, to an outsider, especially a Qadirian, our capital must look like so much tarnish on a golden crown that once shown brightly.

"Her only pleasure was the palace gardens. She used to make many sketches of what she saw there. In her search for arresting views she discovered many of the statues that are hidden within, lost to poorly kept shrubbery. How many sketches of these did she make? How many a likeness in pencil or charcoal before she thought to ask about their creator?

"She learned that the sculptor was still alive. Not only that, he lives here in the capital. I have already mentioned him. He is the dwarf, Ottmar, of whom all of Oppara used to speak. He fell out of favor due to his gruff manner, still, he was given a modest pension. He kept himself busy with an epic work to which he'd devoted nearly a decade of research, planning, and modeling. This was a monumental statue depicting one of the Ten Warriors of the Old Mage Jatembe, who brought light and wisdom to a people lost in darkness, so said the bard. Of these ancient things I know little.

"This statue was of the warrior Mataabō, whose steed was a giant lizard that walked on its two powerful hind legs, a type of creature not seen anymore, the size of which would prove preposterous, were we to see it now. Only the gods know if they once truly existed. Well, Ottmar is a perfectionist. He did not wish to imagine his lizard, but to work from life. He sent to the Mwangi Expanse, you've heard of it? No? It's a vast and wild jungle, against which the sharp blade of civilization has made no cut since Jatembe's time.

"A suitable specimen was brought back along with two natives from the expanse who had some understanding of the creature. Mind you, it was no colossal beast." Here Old Khalden laughed. "It must have stood no taller than either of you and a sight narrower, I surmise. It was half bird, for it was feathered about its head and neck. Yet it had the carnivore's dangerous bite and it possessed claws like reaping scythes. It ate meat, which its handlers were quick to give it, lest it leap upon them.

"Ottmar was making a careful study of this bird-lizard. About this time Princess Fatima learned of her favorite sculptor's identity. She sent him a request, desiring to see him. Even though Ottmar's pension was on the line, the request was ignored. He is one of those singleminded artist who cannot take even a modest break from his work. If Fatima was not so timid, that is, if she possessed more of what we'd call the typical attitude of royalty, she would have had Ottmar drug from his studio and thrown down before her. As it was, she sent beseeching letters and plenty of gifts, thinking to earn the dwarf's good grace.

"However, Ottmar remained obsessed with his work. Now, if you recall, Fatima was like a cat that may or may not conquer its fear and approach. She *did* overcome her timidity and one day, quite without warning, appeared in Ottmar's studio. You might imagine he'd be put out but the exact opposite happened. Here was this delicate, timid creature, blown in like a blossom, a treat to his eye and so completely unlike him in demeanor that the dwarven artist fell in love. Not romantic love, mind you, but the love an artist has for something beautiful and pure.

"Ottmar now had to make amends for his rude behavior. He gave Fatima the royal treatment, as it were, showing her his meagre studio and his even more meagre quarters. Even though his tools were old they were made by dwarven hands and thus were of the highest quality. Finally, after so much fumbling through social niceties, the two were accustom to one another. A genuine friendship formed. Many visits followed. In time, when Ottmar was truly comfortable with Fatima, he showed her Mataabō on his feathered steed.

"Would you believe Fatima laughed? Not at the workmanship, which was sublime, but that such a creature existed at all, or ever had. Here, a daughter of the genie-folk, and she doubted the existence of this giant bipedal lizard. Well, if Ottmar wasn't so enchanted with our princess he would have put her out on her rump. Thankfully, he had a better solution. He showed her the lizard from the Mwangi Expanse.

"Now, mind you, this lizard was no household pet. Ottmar had never so much as touched a brightly colored feather on its head. Not even the handlers, born and raised around such a fantastic creature, dare approach it. This glorified chicken scared them all to death. Not Fatima, the very first thing she did was approach it, hand extended. Thankfully, Ottmar drew her back. The lizard, suffering such an affront as it never had, emitted such a threatening hiss, that everyone present fled to safer quarters.

"Grand Prince Stavian could not delay forever. His Uncle wasn't getting any younger. The wedding date was set. You might feel sorry for our princess but fear not, such marriages are more for show than for anything else. Still, her fate was uncertain. What kind of husband would Uncle Hendrik make? The question didn't worry Fatima. She was too involved with her dwarven sculptor, whose platonic love was enthusiastically reciprocated.

"Ottmar decided that his great work would make the perfect wedding present for Fatima. He double his efforts, working from dawn until the wee hours of the night in order to finish the statue in time. His aging body could not endure the work. He fell ill and exhausted and was confined to bed. The wedding date approached but the great statue of Mataabō was not yet complete. What do to? There was no way it could be completed in time without compromising its quality. This Ottmar would not do.

"He decided on a placeholder. He no longer needed the feathered lizard. That part of the statue had been completed. He made a gift of the lizard and of its handlers to the princess. These handlers were pleased, as their pay increased and their living quarters were vastly superior. The lizard too was pleased, for it could now roam the garden outside of the princess's quarters, instead of the sunless yard behind Ottmar's studio.

"These handlers found Fatima and the other personages of the palace a most difficult group. While Ottmar respected the lizard's dangerous qualities, the nobility felt immune to any harm. They had never known anything truly wild. The handlers attempted to communicate the danger involved but were ignored. There were many close calls.

"Now, there was something known to these handlers that was unknown to Ottmar or Fatima. These wise Mwangi tried to express their understanding but somehow they fell short of their goal. What they knew but could not communicate was this; the lizard was young, an adolescent. It was also female. It was rapidly approaching its first season. The females of this particular species are unusually aggressive during their season. They are motivated to go in hunt of a mate. The poor males of this species are practically assaulted. This aggressiveness is most pronounced in the first year, tapering off as the female ages.

"These wise Mwangi attempted to convince the princess to do one of two things before the first season came; have the lizard killed, or have the lizard returned to the expanse. By this time Fatima was quite taken with this death-dealing chicken. She spent hour after hour observing and sketching it. She could not comprehend the warning given by the lizard's handlers. When they grew more insistent she grew offended. In her naivety she had them dismissed. They went to Ottmar but found him so ill, exhausted, and listless as to be almost insensible. These poor Mwangi had no recourse but to pray to the gods, take their gold, and return home.

"Just about the time Ottmar was returning to health the lizard was coming into her first season. The princess was asleep one night when she heard a most disturbing sound. It was a mournful wailing, a mixture of a scream and a funeral dirge. Although the sound woke her and she heard it still, she thought she was dreaming, for the sound belonged more rightly to the realm of nightmares.

"She followed this sound into her private garden and there found the feathered-lizard curled up in the moonlight, moaning most pitifully. The lizard turned its plaintive eyes on the princess. The pain and anguish of the beast's gaze wounded the princess's sensitive heart. She had no idea of the danger she was in, for the mournful sound was one side of a coin whose other side was rage. The princess, desiring to console the lizard, approached, knelt, and reached out." Here Old Khalden stopped. He could hear the pounding hearts before him and the strain of lungs whose air was held tight.

"Afterwards, the lizard was put to death. The princess—buried in her private garden. A day of mourning was called. Her funeral train stretched across Oppara. This was some time ago, mind you. Perhaps you are too young to remember it? As it so happened, for at times the gods can be cruel, Ottmar had labored with renewed vigor and was near to completing the statue of Mataabō. When he heard of Fatima's death he struck deeply the face of that ancient hero, dropped his chisel and hammer, and once more fell ill, this time of heartbreak.

"Well," said Old Khalden, "this is but one half of our story. For you wished to know of this statue's origins. You have heard of the life and death of Fatima, yes, but there is more to hear about Ottmar. The night grows long and the air cold. I hear my bed calling. Do not yet buy raspberry tarts for your teacher but stay in her ill-favor so that we may speak tomorrow night." With this Old Khalden surprised the two youths by passing through the hidden entrance, the *Order of Numbers* tucked under his arm.

. . .

"Ah," said Old Khalden, the blind beggar-thief, when the two young apprentices returned to his mat. This time he was prepared for them. A wicker basket was at his left hand. The *Order of Numbers* at his right. He brought the basket around and motioned for the boys to partake of its contents. "Mara was most please to sell all of her tarts before they'd even cooled." He held up a finger. "Do leave a few for your poor instructor. How she labors!" The two boys laughed. He had also a bottle of goat's milk. He set this next to the basket. He knew that boys of any temperament can be pacified and pleased by such things as pastries and milk. It was in this way he found a most agreeable audience.

"Now we must speak of Ottmar, whose fate is perhaps worse than Fatima's. How? Who knows what charity the gods give to those innocent, young princesses who come before them? As for those who've grown cynical by time's many injuries—" He shrugged his shoulders.

"Should they expect Heaven after this? Eh? But these are matters for philosophers and priests.

"When we left Ottmar he was bed-ridden, ill of heart. He dismissed his assistants and barred the door of his studio. He could not bear to see Mataabō's feathered lizard, nor the gash that marred that noble warrior's face, for this very wound mirrored the one that cut through Ottmar's soul. You see, he blamed himself for Fatima's death. To mourn is to wrestle with the hard truths of time.

"With Fatima's death his pension was ended. Uncle Hendrik blamed the sculptor too. He even called for the dwarf's execution. Grand Prince Stavian, despite all his evil instincts, hates the sight of blood. Exile? requested Uncle Hendrik. Eh, let it go, said the Grand Prince. And so the world forgot about Ottmar. Both studio and home fell into neglect and disrepair. Animals found their way in, pushing their heads through holes and making nests within Mataabō's crevices and within arms-reach of the once lauded artist.

"What does soul-sickness do to a man? It's misery. Artists, too, are perhaps more vulnerable to such corrosive states. Is it any wonder that Ottmar began to lose his hold on reality? He began to speak to the rats and crows. He gave them his bread, he subsisting on crumbs. Isolation does strange things to a man, believe me. One gets to talking to beasts as if they'd answer. In time, one believes they do!

"One crow in particular adopted Ottmar. Crows, as you know, are intelligent. They have poor manners, yes, but they are smart enough to recognize a good thing when it comes along."

"They know their mark," said Eshkol.

"Yes," agreed Khalden. "This crow figured out that if it stood on the headboard or on Ottmar himself, as he lie under the covers, it got first choice of whatever food was available. Soon this crow chased off its competition. The rats were pecked and squawked at until they went in search of a more peaceful abode. The other crows were harder to dislodge, but, as this enterprising crow grew fat, it was able to oust all others through sheer muscle.

"So, after a season or two we find Ottmar and his crow living like wizard and familiar. Perhaps the following is only the bard's fancy, or perhaps it is truth, who can say? But, this crow, having grown fond of its benevolent provider, or perhaps scheming for more food, realized that an active dwarf is better than an inactive one. This crow began to work on Ottmar. How? It found its way into his studio, no doubt through some hole in the roof. It managed to carry tool after tool from the studio into the house, and drop them noisily on the floor by Ottmar's bed.

"Can you imagine it? What must have Ottmar thought when confronted by the rude persistence of this remarkable bird? Tool after tool, even those whose weight you would think prevented such transport, made their way from studio shelf to Ottmar's bedside. 'What, damn you?' I can imagine the consternated dwarf demand. This crow, and here we begin to mistrust our bard, even in a world such as this, answered.

"It scolded its protector and provider. 'Enough is enough,' it said. 'Back to work with you!'" Said Old Khalden. "Can you imagine it? Eh, there are stranger things. Even dwarves must acknowledge that the occasional crow will talk. 'But what?' Asked Ottmar of his supernatural advisor. 'Fatima!' Answered the crow.

"You see, this crow had been paying attention—listening to Ottmar's lamentations. While man confuses himself with his vast intellect, beasts get right to the issue. The only cure for Ottmar's soul-sickness, knew this wily old crow, was forgiveness. How could Ottmar forgive himself? As a dwarf he must look to stone and to his hands. As a sculptor—well, the answer is obvious.

"Ottmar could hardly grasp what this impertinent crow demanded of him. It was too much for his pained heart. Have you ever tried to keep a crow from a bit of carrion? Kick or scream or throw rocks, they hop about or maybe take flight, but return they will. Before long Ottmar couldn't turn back his blanket, so heavy was it with tools. Nor could he occupy himself with sobbing or painful introspection without getting a motivating peck. What the crow lacked in subtlety it more than made up for in obnoxious persistence. In time Ottmar found himself prying loose the boards over his studio door.

"I'm too crude a man to know how that first vision of Mataabō and his lizard mount must have struck Ottmar. If I know the dwarven character, even that of an artist, once a dwarf takes a tool in-hand, sentimentality is banished. So began the statue you see behind you. This great hero and his lizard mount had one last service to man, for locked within that stone was Fatima, a likeness that belies belief, or so I hear said.

"Ottmar worked as a man possessed. All the while the crow watched. Chunks of stone were split away, falling with a crash. Mataabō must have known his fate, for he surrendered without protest. In the heart of his lizard mount was the stone that would provide a delicate yet enduring beauty. Fatima," Khalden smiled, "Fatima was there. Ottmar revealed her.

"The statue seemed to carve itself. It's like that sometimes, I imagine. Ottmar stood back one day, hammer and chisel in-hand, and stopped. He knew the statue was done, needing only to be polished. He set aside his tools and wept, not tears of sadness, no, tears of joy. He had created a masterpiece. It was as if Fatima was standing before him. His moment of glory was interrupted, however, for the crow was hopping about and making such a racket as to shatter even a dwarf's pleased tranquility.

"'What, damn you?' Asked Ottmar. 'Jewels!' Cried the crow. 'Jewels!' Ottmar looked at the statue and searched his memory. He turned to the crow. 'She never wore jewelry, you—' But the cry of 'jewels, jewels', continued without cease. Ottmar thought. Yes, he realized, at the wedding, and everyday thereafter, she would have had fantastic jewels. He had never seen them. He gazed for a long time at his squawking companion. He turned to the statue. How, he asked himself, could he add jewels he'd never seen?

"The crow read his mind. 'Stavian,' it said, 'Stavian.'" Here Khalden paused. He had spoken at length and was thirsty. He felt for the bottle of milk. Owen understood what the blind beggar wished, took his hand, and placed within it the bottle.

"We've saved the rest for you," he said.

"A tart, too," said Eshkol.

"Kind boys," said Khalden. He held out the bottle with one hand, wiping his chin with the other. Owen took the bottle. Khalden did not yet eat the sweet treat, but continued his tale.

"Ottmar went to the castle. He requested an audience with the Grand Prince. It took some time for the prince to recall the name Ottmar. When he did he was curious. He assumed the dwarf wished to resume his pension. People were always beseeching him for gold. He was surprised when Ottmar enquired not about money, but about Fatima's jewels. After some confusion and a great deal of attention to security, they were produced.

"Ottmar was escorted into a dining room. One wall of this room was comprised of windows opening to a lovely garden of fruit trees. Word had gotten around that

Fatima's jewels were being retrieved from the royal treasury. The maids, who normally stayed out of sight, determined that those windows must be washed on that day. Two maids stood within the dining room, one outside. They opened the windows and gossiped while they cleaned. Each had her head turned in order to catch a glance at the jewels. The swift breeze of the Inner Sea carried the scent of the fruit blossoms into the room.

At one end of the long table, set out on rich velvet, were the princess's wedding jewels. A guard stood beside the table. A man, associated with the royal treasury, was standing behind the table. Ottmar began to take measurements and sketch out the details of each piece.

"As Ottmar examined the pieces, the treasury-man rattled off the history of each. The twin, lime-green stones, with their milky swirls, set in platinum earrings were from Kyonin. They had come from the tomb of an elven queen. The bracelet had been found in an excavation in Sargava. The stones, which resembled frozen flames, could not be identified and were considered unique. The necklace, and here the treasury-man spoke with marked pride—the maids ceased cleaning all together and listened with rapt attention—was not only an emerald of perfect color and clarity, it possessed an enchantment by none other than Nex himself, or so it was determined, such things are damnably hard to verify. What was the enchantment? None knew. No amount of divination could reveal it. The magic of that immortal wizard was far too advanced to give up its secrets, especially to the ignoramuses who probed and prodded like children. How to activate the enchantment? Ask Nex.

"Each piece," continued Khalden, "was befitting the princess that Ottmar had come to love. He finished his sketches and was half out of the door, the treasury-man donning his silk gloves, the guard looking forward to his lunch-feast, the maids deciding that the windows were sparkling, when there came a sudden flapping sound; wings at close quarters. Ottmar ducked and scrambled through the open door. The guard reached for his sword. The treasury-man reached for the jewels. He was rewarded with a blood-drawing peck on his forearm.

"The crow who had demanded, 'Jewels! Jewels!', materialized. This mysterious bird had been waiting to pounce. You see, it had been present the entire time, having waddled into the room on Ottmar's heels. It had stood in the corner, seen by none, for all attention went to the jewels. When Ottmar finished, this thief, yes, for this bird is as we are, avaricious to the core, leapt upon the table. It grabbed the Nex-enchanted necklace, turned its gaze this way and that, rocked a bit like crows do, then launched and flapped over the heads of the screaming maids. The last sight of that necklace, whose value was inestimable, was its jump through an open window, carried in the glossy black claws of the crow.

"Ottmar was seized at once, drug to the dungeon, and interrogated. His story was told to the Grand Prince, who, would you believe, laughed until tears came. He had the guard and the treasury-man thrown into the dungeon. Ottmar, he released, on one condition: the statue of Fatima was to be gifted to the crown, to make up for that priceless artifact which had flown away. His sense of justice, or was it irony, was most unique.

"Now we have arrived at the end of our tale, my young friends. The statue, which even the daft Grand Prince acknowledges as a work of sublime beauty and unequaled craftsmanship, was far too remarkable to remain out of public sight. So," Khalden motioned to the statue, "there stands Fatima. As for Ottmar—"

But Old Khalden's words were interrupted by a sharp click, nails on stone. He turned his ear to the source.

Eshkol and Owen turned to look behind them. There appeared to be no source of the odd sound. Then, as the boys watched, a crow materialized from the deeper darkness, standing atop Fatima. It held in its black beak a delicate necklace, a platinum chain with a flawless emerald. It lowered its head and slipped the necklace around Fatima's slender neck.

"What is it, boys?" whispered Old Khalden.

"The crow," whispered Eshkol.

"What's it doing?" asked Khalden.

"It's got the necklace!" cried Owen.

The crow, which was no ordinary bird, but was some sort of wicked fey or the results of an ancient wizard's troublesome meddling, which, was more commonly called a "witchcrow," turned its black eyes to the seated group of fellow thieves. More intelligence shown within those dark orbs than any natural crow, or indeed, most men, possessed. It extended its wings and fluttered down to the base of the statue. It turned its gaze upwards and seemed to regard the effect the necklace had when paired with Ottmar's masterpiece.

"Owen," whispered Khalden, "club that wicked thing. Eshkol, grab the necklace before it's too late."

As Khalden spoke these words, the witchcrow began to hop and dance. It spat out such unnerving sounds that the two young thieves were slow to act. Old Khalden, more experienced, and therefore less easily dissuaded, threw back the cover of the *Order of Numbers* and plucked out his enchanted dagger. He rose and began to creep toward the racket. When he stepped between Eshkol and Owen they were awoken from their stupor and took to their feet. The witchcrow continued its bizarre dance.

Just as Khalden was within striking distance the witchcrow stopped, turned toward him, and gave a shrill squawk of such menacing pitch that the blind beggar and his two compatriots were stopped. The witchcrow took flight, landed on Fatima's head, bent, plucked the necklace free, then rose up to its full height. It gave the trio the evil eye, nodded its head three times in rapid succession, and disappeared from sight. Only Old Khalden could hear the flapping of its wings as it passed over them.

The trio stood for some time in silence. Eshkol and Owen looked at one another. Old Khalden had his ear turned skyward, a wry smile on his face. Once he was certain the witchcrow was gone and the evening's excitement was through he yawned, stretched, and made his way back to his mat. He crouched, felt for the *Order of Numbers,* found it, and stood.

"Well, boys," he said, replacing his dagger within the holy book and shutting the cover. "A finer ending could not have been had. A master thief that was!" He laughed, turned, and headed toward the secret entrance to the Brotherhood of Silence's headquarters. He paused, turned, and smiled at the two boys. "Leave my raspberry tart out for the birds. One never knows," he said, his voice echoing from the shadows. "One never knows."

Three Familiars

"Magic?" asked Brunhilda, a dwarf, and therefore suspicious of the arcane. She knelt over the rigid body of Remus, found the closeness uncomfortable, stood and stepped to her deputy. He was a young man, until recently a shepherd, named Elgin. His patience and his powers of observation had recommended him to Brunhilda, the Sheriff of Hausswolffen, of which Elgin was natural born, she having come down from Battlewall.

Remus had once been a tutor to White Estrid, the King of Halgrim (the title of King was applied no matter the gender) and therefore an inquiry was being made, whereas the superstitious locals might have otherwise boarded up the tower and called its environs haunted, never to be trespassed.

"A letter," said Elgin. "He must have been writing it when he died. See?" He pointed to the smudged ink in the lower right-hand corner, which had transferred itself to the wizard's cheek, indicating a sudden loss of consciousness. Brunhilda turned, as the wizard was crumpled on the carpet, having slid out of his chair, presumably upon dying.

"The papers bear tracks," said Elgin.

Brunhilda examined what appeared to be paw prints. "An animal's."

"You think he was killed by an animal?"

"Doubtful," she said. "Eh, it's small, judging from the size. Most likely a pet. It must have jumped up on the desk while he was writing." Her thoughts returned to Remus. "Perhaps it was something in the paper. Something he unknowingly triggered, a trap," she said. "Wizards make the craftiest assassins."

"Murder?"

Brunhilda looked down at Remus. "He's not so old. Doesn't look ill." She glanced at her deputy. "There's no marks on him." She looked around the study. "No signs of struggle." She began to pace. "I'm not the right person for this. Damn the riddle that is magic," she said, slamming a fist into an open palm.

"Sven Seven-Eyes is on the way," said Elgin.

"Three days, if Gozreh wills it," said Brunhilda, looking down at Remus.

Elgin had nothing to add.

"Let's look at this letter," she said. "If you're certain it isn't trapped."

"Trapped?"

"With runes, or—how should I know?"

Elgin looked over the pages. "Seems to be plain writing, Sheriff."

"Let's hope."

. . .

"What can I say to you, my friend?" Began the letter. "I left in haste, without farewell, and with doubt in my heart as to the continuation of our friendship. With the application of that universal salve—time—and with it, logic regaining rule over emotion, I've come to doubt my own perceptions. To make sense of my actions I shall speak of events of which you are unawares and with which, I hope, you shall find cause for forgiveness.

"As you well know it was on account of Agatha, my faithful familiar. She had somehow fallen ill. Cats are wont to catch a bug now and again. I thought perhaps it was the persistent draft in this old tower. If only I could give Agatha a change of scenery.

"What other reason did I need to travel south? It had been years, had it not? Each of us lost in our research, me sorting through the intricacies of enchantment, and you, my once fellow apprentice, familiarizing yourself with those ever-varied denizens of the outer planes. Besides, this tower is too isolated. It was a gift, you know, from my patron and protector, the King. The sea is my neighbor and the winds blow without cease, putting a dreadful cold into these gray stones.

"I set out and you greeted me, if not with the cordiality I had hoped for, then with excitement about your work; which, amongst our kind, is contagious. I must admit, some of your recent 'breakthroughs' alarmed me. Do you not remember what that curmudgeon, Valstaf, said about the Abyss, staring in and what not? Well, it isn't my place to lecture.

"The climate along Lake Encarthan was a welcome change. Even Agatha perked up. Of course, the mice in your tower stepped lively to give her a bit more exercise than she's accustom to. (My own mice are languid.) As you know, I planned to spend the winter there. I lasted but a fortnight. What must you have thought when you found your guest quarters empty?

"Did you think that I took offense at how little time we had spent in conversation or in shared magical exploration? No, my friend, I well know how a caster's mind works. Time is of the least concern, lest it be time wasted, then we balk. Socializing is not far behind. I was to occupy myself with that tome you have on the crafting of ioun stones. (Shall I yet have that pleasure?)

"As you know Agatha took to you with great curiosity, following you everywhere, butting against your calves when you stopped. I swear she lost a few pounds in her relentless shadowing of you. She even, on occasion, slept in your chambers, or perhaps stayed up to watch you work. I am so used to her lying just behind my knees at night that her absence struck me as a phantom limb. Her behavior was unusual but I took it to be a bit of the animating spirit of youth, brought on, I surmise, by the cat-and-mouse game.

"What was the cause of my rude departure? There's nothing for it but to relate matters as they happened. As I mentioned, Agatha had taken up spying on you. On this particular night she was not in bed with me. Later, I was awoken by her meowing. I brought up a light and saw her in the doorway. She must have come to check on me. Finding me whole and in the expected place she dashed off. I dispelled my light and returned to sleep.

"Before I had quite come under Desna's influence I was awoken again by Agatha, this time climbing into bed. She was less talkative than usual, which I took to be exhaustion, and—again out of character—she wanted under the covers. I obliged her and succumbed at once to slumber. I awoke, as men of our age do, in the middle of the night, and felt for Agatha. She was no longer in bed. Also, her spot was cold. She must not have stayed long.

"I was a bit worried. I called for her but she didn't come. One knows how tied we wizards are to our familiars. I concentrated and began to sense that something was amiss. I went in search of her, calling out her name. I came to your study door, found it closed, yet saw light beneath. I knocked, but you must not have heard. I admit that I knelt and attempted to spy through the keyhole, but saw nothing. I admit also to getting down on my hands and knees and calling Agatha's name through the gap.

"She came rushing to the door, meowing, and attempting to stick her nose beneath. When that failed she reached under, not in that playful-predatory way cats do, but as a drowning man might reach for the aid of one in a raft. I touched her paw to let her know I was present. I spoke soothingly to her, but alas, I could hear in the troubled warble of her meows that she was scared out of her wits.

"I do not believe you have a familiar, so you may not know that one's attachment becomes such that man can understand beast, vice versa. I asked Agatha what had so shocked her. She was, at first, unable to organize her admittedly simple thoughts. After being somewhat calmed by my voice she was able to communicate her impressions. It was obvious that she had no comprehension of what she had witnessed, save for the animal's instinctive understanding of danger. This troubled me. I caught a bit of the panic that gripped her.

"I rose and banged on your door. No response. I pulled the handle to no effect. I remembered a scroll of knocking amongst my processions and went to get it. I returned and read it, a transgression against you, but Agatha's plaintive cries spurred me to such rash behavior. Much to my surprise the door did not budge. That is quite unusual and quite worrisome.

"Were you in trouble? Had one of your summons gone awry? Had you stared too long into the Abyss and were suffering the consequences? There was one last recourse available. Those with long ties to their familiars are able to scry upon them. I set myself outside of your door, concentrated, and focused my mind's eye upon my frightened familiar.

"I was able to see her and around her the flagstones of your study floor, beyond that, all was fog. I concentrated with greater effort and the fog was partially dispelled. Only the edge of your carpet revealed itself. I spoke to Agatha, encouraging her to find you. She refused, something she had never done, being courageous, or, perhaps, by default, curious. I commanded her and she reluctantly turned and went off in search of you. My vision, centered on her, and still clouded, added little information.

"Agatha halted and began to meow. She would go no further, despite my command, and despite the risk of raising my ire. She then began to hiss, arch her back, and raise her fur against something I could not see. She had not made it far from the door. I heard your approach. I saw your form appear at the edge of the fog. I then heard you speaking to Agatha. Despite your attempts to soothe her she remained agitated. Knowing you were close to the door I broke off my scrying, rose, and knocked.

"You opened the door, after a suspiciously long delay. There you stood, Agatha in your arms. I was surprised to see this, given her previous state of alarm. You were not, however, surprised to see me. I informed you of my search for Agatha, at which time you placed her in my arms. We said goodnight and I returned to my quarters. I could detect nothing of your work, though I looked eagerly over your shoulder.

"Agatha was dazed and exhausted. The two of us went to bed, but, I admit, neither of us slept. I could not feel her mind. Nor could I encourage her to voice her thoughts. She remained distant and silent, staring into the darkness through half-opened eyes.

"There is a spell, rare and difficult to cast, but known to me, in which one can 'read' the memories of one's familiar. It can be a dangerous spell in that it is easy to become trapped in an animal's thoughts, for they are so repetitive and of such a simple, immediate nature that to remember the self and return to the self can sometimes elude the caster.

"Despite the risk, I cast this spell and investigated not only that one night's events but all of Agatha's memories as they related to you. They were patchy and confused, but here I no longer speak of events unknown to you, for you know well what Agatha witnessed.

"While I may have moral qualms about making contact with that realm beyond knowing, I hesitate to condemn you. We all explore, in our own way, those mysteries that grip our imaginations. Still, whatever knowledge you seek by questioning the *Qlippoth*—for what else could such an indescribably monstrosity be—and what sense you are able to make of their answers, can it be worth the risk?

"Perhaps I behaved rashly or perhaps seeing Agatha in that state affected me, but I decided that the healing balm of a change of place had become instead a harm and, I worried, a disease of the mind, for the *Qlippoth* can derange a mind as easily as they can illuminate one (indeed, they may think those two disparate activities one and the same).

"I left that morning without confronting you.

"Agatha remained in her shocked state for days afterwards. I admit, I blamed you, and held a grudge. Now that we are home and she has her obliging mice at hand, or rather paw, I hope she shall come around. I take her current fatigue and listlessness to be the repercussions of stress and travel. I have faith she will fully recover.

"As I said, I have given the entire episode some thought and I must apologize. I—

"It's as far as he got, eh?" asked Brunhilda. She looked to Elgin. "What's a—" She glanced again at the letter, and being unable—or afraid—to pronounce the name, pointed at it.

Elgin made an attempt. "Qlip-poth?" He shrugged his shoulders. "Maybe Sven will know."

Brunhilda looked around the study. "No Agatha."

"Cats hide," said Elgin.

"Cats *do* hide," said Brunhilda. "We had better find her. Maybe Sven knows that spell Remus spoke of."

"Her memories?" asked Elgin.

"Aye."

. . .

"No," said Sven Seven Eyes, three days later (Gozreh *had* willed it).

"Damn," said Brunhilda. "Would've been useful."

Sven's laughter caused her to arch her brows.

"If it's in one of his spell books, I'll know it soon enough." He pulled back the tattered edge of his robe, revealing an ermine, that is, a white-furred weasel. "What a treat to read *your* thoughts," he said to his own familiar. The ermine looked up at him as if daring his master to attempt it. Sven turned to Brunhilda. "Where's the cat?"

"Must still be in the tower. We never did find her."

"And his spell books?" asked Sven.

"In his library."

"Well, let us find this frightened cat," he said. He looked to his familiar. "A new friend for you. Do restrain your play. She's been through a lot."

. . .

Brunhilda unlocked the tower. The trio entered, Sven leading the way. "Rather drafty in here." He observed. "Sure he didn't die of exposure?"

"Wasn't this bad before," said Elgin.

The trio arrived (four, if you count the ermine, as all wizards would) outside of the study. A pronounced wind whistled through the partially open door. Sven pushed it open. "A shame," he said, stepping to the center of the room. He knelt and looked over Agatha. Brunhilda and Elgin peered over his shoulders.

Agatha lay in the exact spot where her master had died (his body having been removed), stretched out on her side. Her front paws were black with ink. Her stomach hung open, her viscera spilled out onto the carpet. An orange slime mingled with her blood. Her eyes were open and if it were possible to judge a cat's final thoughts by the cast of its death-stilled face, Agatha's was that of relief.

The trail of slime crossed the carpet to a shattered window, through which a swirl of snow blew. Halfway between Agatha and the window was a second pile of viscera. Sven rose, walked to it, and knelt. "A cast-off skin." He turned and glanced at Agatha. "A *second* cast-off skin." He picked it up and examined it. "Like that of a squid, albeit with tiny bat's wings." He set it down, rose, and walked to the window, peering out. He turned to Brunhilda and Elgin, "We'll need a different spell." He looked at Agatha. "Speak with the dead."

Three Worshippers

In hole—like you say. Nude. Ground moist—moving—biting. Big moon up. Made eyes hurt. Now, little lights. Never knew about little lights—Oh! Voices!

"Why couldn't we talk inside?"

Woman—not dwarf—like me. I tell—not sound like Mamma. Elf?

Woman: "And why come here, of all places, and at this unholy hour?"

"Walls have ears."

A man. Know voice? Can't remember—

Man: "Besides, I want to do something for you."

Woman: "Start by giving me your robe, I'm cold."

She need blanket like mine—alive—warm—hungry.

Man: "Use a spell."

Woman: "I didn't ask Calistra for that particular spell."

Man laugh at funny name.

Man: "Ah, here we are. A friend of yours?"

Woman: "Amir Magus?"

Sound like read aloud. Mamma read to me—when I young. I like. She read stories of heroes. She tell when we fight gods. They make us go into rocks. Good thing, say Mamma. We like rocks better. Mamma say gods can have sky. Mamma say sky no good—no ore in sky. Never heard Mamma say funny word woman say. Name? Sound like name hear before—can't remember.

Man: "I saw you at the service."

Woman: "No, you didn't."

She terse. I learn word. I tell people terse. Mamma terse. She taught word.

Man: "Come now, disguise self is a paltry illusion. You didn't have the discipline to stick with the arcane, did you? That's why you switched over. Faith is easier, perhaps? Especially a faith that involves so much—"

Woman: "If you brought me out here to insult me —"

Man: "Amir was a worshipper of Calistra, wasn't he?"

Woman: "No, he was a hypocrite and a betrayer."

She unhappy. She cold still. I give her blanket—when I done. You say use every night—even if not cold or tired. You say worms hungry. Bite so much!

Man: "Yet, here he lies, in the graveyard of the temple of Abadar."

Woman: "Yes, *your* temple. I know."

Man: "Why is he here?"

Woman: "I've already told you."

Man: "Did you know that Magus left a substantial part of his estate to the church. My church, not your church."

No talk. What they do? Can't hear—down in hole. Get up, Master? Worms full. They no bite so much. Put worms in mouth—to eat—like you want. There. Just like you say. Now—standing—see out—hear better. Don't step on ladder—it talk.

Man: "I suppose he tired of the endless debauchery that Calistra offers. At some point one has to get serious. He seems to have had a change of heart."

Woman: "It happens. Why gloat?"

Man: "What is it that Calistra says about revenge?"

Woman: "Get it."

Man: "You can't 'get it' now, can you? A little late, eh? How does your goddess feel about that?"

Woman: "What makes you think I know?"

Man laugh. Hear before—can't remember. Like name. Should know.

Man: "Pray to her and ask."

Woman no talk. What she do? Me look, Master?

Man: "Then again, maybe that won't work. Seeing as you don't *really* worship her."

Woman: "Excuse me?"

Man: "Let us be honest with one another."

Woman: "I've had enough of this. I should have known better than to have come out here with you."

Her voice get small. Step on ladder. It talk—only a little. They no hear. Can see now. Man close—he look away. Woman mad. She walk.

Man: "We have that in common. As I no longer worship Abadar."

Woman turn. Come back. Don't see me! Get down!

Woman: "What are you talking about?"

Man laugh. He like laugh. Oh, remember! Work for him. He hire me. He give me copper. Dig graves. Copper for you. Under bed. If you need—you have. Okay, Master?

Man: "I began to realize that certain passages in the *Order of Numbers* fascinated me more than others; which, since we're being honest, bored me."

Woman: "And?"

Man: "It dawned on me that what I enjoyed most about Abadar's teachings were the rewards that come from the so-called invisible hand that guides our labors. I wasn't so taken with all the hard work, self-sacrifice, and waiting to get the rewards."

Woman: "So, you're lazy and greedy? I'm not surprised."

Man: "Just as you're lustful. But that isn't what appeals most to you about Calistra, is it?"

Woman: "If you're trying to get at something—"

Man: "How long have we known each other?"

He have bad memory—like me. You help me remember—like to eat worms. Sometimes I can remember on my own—then I feel smart.

Woman: "A decade or more."

Thirsty. Get drink now, Master? Swallow worms—like you say. Have spicy drink. On cart—by pick and shovel. Get out? Want to look at people. Good at climb. Quiet. Remember I quiet, Master? Like when you first show—when I see you.

Remember when they come? They come to see what happen. They think more rocks fall. Master do that. You make rocks fall in cave. You make tunnel. No blame you. Rocks tired—lay down. You dig so much. You no get tired. You say one day I walk—*Spiral Path*. You say—all will. The last day—when you eat all. We walk and you wait at end—wait for us—like worms wait for us. You biggest, hungriest worm. I saw. I know.

Remember? I came alone. I look at tired rocks—to see if they fall and sleep. I good at that. They let me do it. They say I brave. They say I skinny and fast. Not big and slow, like other dwarves. They say a dwarf need to be all of those things when rocks get tired and fall and sleep. I special. They told. No more rocks fall. They come. They see. They scream and cry. They say, I remember, they say:

"Your beard!"

"Your skin!"

"What happened?"

I show you. They mad. They hack—like at ore. I mad. I make stop. I get long worms out, like you say. They fall. They sleep. They quiet. No mad. I leave. Remember? Be quiet, you say. Leave, you say. Remember? You make hair fall out. You make skin like yours. They angry for what you do. They quiet now. Worms eat.

Man: "I've been observing you."

Woman: "Creep."

Man: "Don't flatter yourself."

Woman: "Well—"

Man: "I've noticed that all of your enemies are ruthlessly dispatched, while your lovers are left to linger. That doesn't fit Calistra's teachings. I've noticed that, over the past few years, you've gone out of your way to make new enemies, perhaps to justify expressing your wrath."

Woman: "Or maybe people are rude and sometimes get their comeuppance. Perhaps you should choose your words wisely."

Get out hole? Okay? Be quiet. I drink—hide—watch.

Man: "Eiseth."

New funny name.

Man: "Ah, I can tell by your expression that the name holds meaning for you. A Queen of the Night, I believe, yes? What are her particular obsessions? Battle, revenge—wrath?"

Woman: "Damn you."

She stand close to man.

Woman: "How—"

Man: "Like any usurer, Mammon has no mercy for those who owe him debts. He's had cause to appeal to Eiseth. Such alliances work in Hell, why not here?"

They quiet. Get clothes now, Master? Man and woman funny. They look—no talk. Why? Touch lips? No—no touch lips.

Woman: "How long have you known?"

Man: "Long enough. Don't worry, your secret is safe with me. Besides, I'm not overly eager to anger one of Eiseth's followers. Is my secret safe with you?"

Woman: "I suppose it has to be, doesn't it? Now, if I'm not wrong, you wanted to do something for me?"

Man: "As I said, I saw through your attempts to hide your identity at the service. The look of hatred did nothing to mar the beauty of your face."

Woman: "You could have complimented me indoors."

Man: "Certainly, but I couldn't have divulged the truth, now could I?"

Woman: "Go on."

Man: "I suppose you're not familiar with the funeral rights of Abadar. If you were, you might have noticed that I omitted a few choice phrases, corrupted a few others, and in general, botched the service."

Woman: "No one raised a fuss."

Man: "Oh, after the first few minutes most people stop listening. The living have their own concerns. Even those who attend services regularly haven't quite figured out that some of the new teachings are from Mammon's scripture, not Abadar's. Not that they're overly familiar with the former. Yet, more and more are being converted to the 'new way.' There is a sizable and growing cult to Mammon—regulars in the church."

Woman: "I still don't see the point of all this."

Man: "An alliance. You've shown great skill in dispatching those you dislike. Maybe you can lend your services to a growing church who, despite the obvious benefits of membership, is forced to keep that membership a secret."

She laugh.

Woman: "You don't want to get your hands dirty?"

Man: "Something like that. To show you how generous I can be, I give you Amir Magus. You can have your revenge."

Woman: "I don't get you. He's dead."

Man: "Well, not quite. He's been poisoned. He reposes, yes, not in death, in a coma. All that is required is a bit of—" He pat side. What in pocket? "We had to go through with a burial to ensure the bequeathing of his estate was accomplished."

Woman: "You buried him *alive*?"

Man: "Well—"

Woman: "You're worse than I am."

Man: "You want him or not?"

Woman: "Oh, I want him."

Man: "Do you remember enough of your arcane teachings to read from a scroll? If not, we'll have to use shovels."

Woman: "That's your plan? Trust me to read a scroll or we dig?"

Man: "Well, while the gravedigger has few, if any friends, he might still spill our little secret."

Woman: "Give me the scroll."

Grave—digger? Me! I bury Amir. Ah! I remember. But—oh no. She say funny words. Oh no. Amir. Trouble. Run away? Afraid. Maybe they no dig. I watch. They can't see. Hiding. Woman say funny words. Oh! All the dirt! Flying! She point. Dirt fly over, make big pile.

Man: "Wonderful. I'll fetch the ladder."

He get ladder. Take to new hole. Amir? Will they see? I can't see. Ladder talk. Man opening box in hole. Oh no, he scream. He mad. Woman looking.

Man: "I don't understand."

Woman: "Maybe he did it himself. If I woke up and found myself buried alive I would—"

Man: "He couldn't have. The poison—I don't—"

Oh no. Big trouble. If I— Will they— Help me say the words—please—Master.

Me: "I let the big worm out."

Woman: "What in the Nine Hells—!"

Ladder talk. Man come out of hole.

Man: "You!"

Me: "The worm—inside—the big worm."

Woman upset—back away. She look at me mean. She look like dwarves look when they see me—after you change me. I no like that look.

Man: "What did you do?"

Me: "The—worm—"

Man angry. He reach for weapon. He take from belt. Tip glow. Don't like. He point at me. No! Bad man! Need help. Help!

Me: "Yhidothrus!"

Sorry! Sorry, Master. You say not to say. I scared.

Man: "What did you say?"

Me: "R-R-Ravager Worm."

Stomach hurts. Big worm inside angry.

Man: "It seems my gravedigger has a secret of his own."

Woman: "What did he say? What was it? A name?"

Me: "Yhidothrus."

Man: "A demon lord, one of those brought over from the, ah, previous inhabitants of the Abyss."

Woman: "What's wrong with him?"

Man: "Leprosy?"

Woman: "Is that a dwarf?"

Me: "Dwarf!"

Woman: "I've never seen a dwarf without a beard. It's—Why does he keep— Oh—"

She laugh.

Woman: "The big worm. I get it."

She no afraid. She stand by man.

Woman: "He must be stupid or something. He thinks the intestines are a big worm."

Man: "He's robbed you of your revenge."

Woman: "I guess he'll have to take Amir's place."

Man: "This is a rod of withering. It will weaken him, not kill him. If you'll accept such a worthless worm as a substitute for Amir—"

Woman: "I don't have much choice, do I?"

No! No! Man angry. He hit me! Ugh. Feel funny tingle. I strong. You make me strong—because I ate worms. Green light no hurt. He bad man. He no do what he did. Bad man! Let his worm out! Use knife. Big worm come out. He try keep in. Woman scream. She no weapon. She looks at green-light-thingy. She look at me. She run. I brave, and skinny, and fast. Not slow, like others. Tackle her.

She wiggly. I hold on. I strong. Turn over. Ugh. She hit. She claw. She bite. She bad, like man. I let big worm out. Good. Come out. No more mean words. No more mean look. They make sad sounds. Now they quiet. They sleep—like dwarves who hit you. Worms free. What now, Master? Put in hole? Put dirt?

You say worms eat. You say feed worms. I do. Keep bad man's stick? Hurt people—if need to. Trouble now? I let big worms out—like with dwarves—in cave with sleeping rocks. You say, no go home. You say, leave—be quiet and leave. Leave now, Master?

Yhidothrus: *Yes.*

Afterward

I hope you enjoyed these stories. If you have, and if you want more, please check out *Breaking the Reign of the Dead*, a novel set in Geb, Nex, and the Mana Waste. You'll find it on Amazon in Kindle, paperback, and hardback versions.

If you enjoy my writing and want still more check out my website, hradbethlen.com or search for me on Amazon. If you think my writing worth sharing please tell a friend.

Thanks for reading.

H. Rad Bethlen has been compared to Isak Dinesen (*Seven Gothic Tales*) and Fritz Leiber (*Ill Met in Lankhmar*). He is known for his work in the fantasy and horror genres as well as his non-fiction. He has been published in Europe and America.

For more great fiction and non-fiction please visit:

roosterandravenpublishing.com

hradbethlen.com

or H. Rad Bethlen's Amazon page.

www.ingramcontent.com/pod-product-compliance
Lightning Source LLC
LaVergne TN
LVHW011031110826
845149LV00015B/3380

* 9 7 8 1 9 6 5 6 5 0 5 3 0 *